OTHER BOOKS BY EDIE RAMER

Contemporary
CRAZY SEXY LOVE (Rescued Hearts, Book 3)
CHRISTMAS AT ANGEL LAKE (Rescued Hearts, Book 2)
HEARTS IN MOTION (Rescued Hearts, Book 1)
MUST WORSHIP CATS (Miracle Interrupted, the beginning)
STARDUST MIRACLE (Miracle Interrupted, Book 2)
MIRACLE LANE (Miracle Interrupted, Book 3)
MIRACLE PIE (Miracle Interrupted, Book 4)
MO'S HEART (Miracle Interrupted, Book 5)
YOU'VE GOT MURDER co-written with Karin Tabke

Paranormal
CATTITUDE
DEAD PEOPLE
DRAGON BLUES

Science Fiction Romance
GALAXY GIRLS
MIXING IT UP (a Galaxy Girls novella)

Short Stories
The Fat Cat (a Cattitude short story)
Dead People in Love (a Dead People short story)
The Kiss (a Galaxy Girls short story)
The Seventh Dimension

For updates, sign up for the Edie's newsletter:
http://edieramer.com/newsletter/

Christmas at Angel Lake
Edie Ramer
Blue Walrus Books
Copyright © 2013 by Edie Ramer
All rights reserved

ISBN-13: 978-1939328113
ISBN-10: 193932811X

Christmas at Angel Lake

Rescued Hearts, Book 2

Edie Ramer

Blue Walrus Books

1

Maddie Barrymore was lost—in more ways than one. She squinted out the window of her beat-up Ford as the wipers swished back and forth, the snow piling up on the sides of the windshield. She should be turning into her sister Kris's driveway right about now, but she'd missed the expressway exit then needed to figure out where she was. Her cell phone wasn't working here, and when her boyfriend had slithered out of their Chicago apartment while she was waitressing, he'd taken with him everything of value, including her GPS system.

Her grip tightened on the steering wheel. Later, she would beat herself up over her lousy choices in men. Right now, she had to concentrate on driving through a near blizzard. Snow-blanketed trees lined the winding road, and she was thankful that at least Kris and her family lived in a city, though its biggest business was a furniture company that made people and cat furniture.

Wonderful. She was moving from a city almost as well known for its cultural center as its crooked politicians to a city known for cat furniture.

And she'd never been that crazy about cats. Except kittens, of course. Something about their small bodies and big, needy eyes and—

A tiny animal darted in front of her car. Her instinct was to slam down on the brakes, but at the last moment, she held back, her booted foot light on the brake pedal. The car swerved toward the animal instead of away from it. As if her thought about cats had conjured it, she thought it was a kitten.

Every muscle in her body rigid, she jerked her foot off the brake and turned the wheel slightly, praying beneath her breath, "Please, don't hit it. Please, please, please."

The car glided into the driveway that had been hidden by shaggy, snow-covered bushes, and she didn't feel any bump.

"Thank you," she whispered, pressing gently on the brake again.

Instead of stopping, the car slid toward the ditch at the edge of the driveway. The front tire on the driver's side dipped into the ditch—and then dipped in farther. As the car tilted to a forty-five-degree angle, she held her breath and clutched the steering wheel.

The car stopped and shuddered. Maddie's breath shuddered, too. Her movements jerky, her left shoulder squashed against the driver's door, she put the car into park, pulled the keys out, then took her shaking, mittened hands off the steering wheel. They still shook as she released the seat belt. And they shook as she slowly lifted her butt over the stick between the two seats—a feat that required twisting her body into the air at awkward angles and leaning on one foot.

She made it to the other seat then tumbled out of the car, falling to her knees in a foot of snow while icy pellets stung her face. She scrambled up...and saw the small cat, ginger and white, at the edge of the road. Not just a cat, either. A kitten. And if she was clenching her teeth to keep them from chattering, the kitten must be nearly frozen.

"Don't run away." Her voice quivered from the cold, each word showing in white puffs. "I'll take care of you."

The kitten meowed, the sound high and sad, and Maddie didn't want to think of what had happened to the animal's mom or brothers and sisters. Maybe they were safe somewhere, and this little one had wandered off and gotten lost.

"I won't hurt you." She crouched and scooped the kitten up. It wiggled in Maddie's mittens. Though she'd just gotten out of the car, the yarn was already damp with snow.

Holding the kitten with one hand, she slid down her oversized zipper and snuggled the kitten down beneath her jacket and her sweater, feeling the cold, snow-covered fur on her breasts. She shivered again but kept an arm against her coat, using it as a shelf for the shivering kitten.

"Let's see if someone at the house can help," she said, feeling doubtful as she gazed at the unplowed driveway. But the snow had come down so quickly. Maybe a plow would come later. She'd come from a military family. Being raised in temporary homes the first twelve years of her life—before the loose ties of her family had finally unraveled—she didn't know a lot about long driveways that needed to be plowed.

But one thing she did know about was making do. And facing the enemy. And going forward, one step at a time.

She took that step—then heard a sharp honk.

She whipped around, squinting at the SUV stopped across the end of the driveway, the window rolling down. Cupping her hand over her jacket to steady the kitten, Maddie headed toward it, moving carefully on the slippery surface. She couldn't fall. It might hurt the kitten.

"I hadn't heard anyone was staying here." A woman peered out of the car's open window, her eyes bright with curiosity. She looked to be in her early fifties, with short, curly, brown hair, puffy cheeks, a double chin, and skin the color of light chocolate. "Is something wrong with your chest?"

"It's a kitten," Maddie said. "I slid into the ditch trying to avoid her. She was freezing, so I put her inside my jacket."

"You must be a cat lover." The woman beamed at her, so Maddie gave a weak smile. The first rule of waitressing—if you wanted to be tipped well—was to let the customer believe what she wanted to believe.

"My cell phone won't work here," Maddie said. "I need to have my car towed—"

"I'll call Dexter to tow it out. My husband. Were you in the house yet?"

"No, I just— Ouch." She looked down, as if she could see through her jacket, at the skin where the kitten had just pricked her.

"You have suitcases?" the woman asked. Not waiting for Maddie's answer, she said, "Get them, and I'll drive you and the kitten to the house. Thank God the heat is on to keep the pipes from bursting, though Dexter doesn't understand why the owners just don't turn off the water. You'll have to put the temperature up. We keep it at fifty-eight degrees in winter."

Maddie stared at her. She should be telling the woman she wasn't staying here, but the words were stuck in her throat.

The woman laughed heartily. "I'm Alma Young. Dexter and I are the caretakers." She swept her hand out at the long drive. "I wish the law firm had warned us that you were coming. Dexter would've plowed instead of waiting for the snow to stop." Her cheerful expression changed to a scowl. "We did get the notice that the firm is changing its name, merging with another one. I got the feeling it's a big shake-up, and anything we do here is just small fish. Dexter thinks they ignore everything we send them anyway. If something needs to be repaired now, he lets them know, gets it fixed, then sends them the bill. It only happened twice so far, and the owner is lucky we're honest. That's all I've got to say."

"Oh, but—"

"How long are you staying? I hope it's a while. Four years is too long to leave a house empty."

"Four years?" Maddie's teeth chattered.

"You're freezing, and I'm keeping you standing in the snow, yakking your ears off." The woman held out her hands in fuzzy purple gloves. "Give me the cat and get your suitcases. If the snow gets any higher on the driveway, even my SUV will get stuck."

Maddie's mind seemed to be as numb as the tip of her nose. Instead of protesting, she obeyed her as if she were

5

a robot.

As if she was really going to stay in the house.

The house where no one lived.

She hurried to the car, but carefully again, not wanting to fall. She couldn't afford to injure herself now. She shouldn't be doing this, taking advantage of the woman's misconception, but who would it hurt if she stayed here a few days?

Maybe stay a week or two. At least until after Christmas before moving into the unfinished basement of her very pregnant sister's small house. Give her time to think of some way to take care of herself without imposing on her sister and brother-in-law and their two-year-old daughter.

Praying that the car wouldn't tip onto its side, she opened the trunk and pulled out a big suitcase and a medium-sized one. Her furniture was in a consignment store in Chicago. That left her life in these two suitcases.

She threw them in the back of the SUV then climbed into the front seat. In Chicago, she wouldn't get into a car with a stranger, but this wasn't Chicago. It was snowing heavily. Her phone wasn't working. Her car was stuck in a ditch. And she had a kitten that needed a home.

The woman who'd introduced herself as Alma Young said she made tapestries while her husband, a retired mechanic, plowed driveways. In summer, her husband took care of lawns for the summer houses. Once a month, she came in and dusted the MacLeesh house and cleaned the toilets, "to make sure there are no rust stains." She wanted to know if there were going to be any changes in the routine.

As if she were a hand puppet and someone else was putting the words into her mouth, Maddie said, "While I'm here, I'll clean the toilets. No need to mention it to the lawyers."

"Oh, I have to. It wouldn't be right to cheat someone."

"Okay, then I won't clean," Maddie said. Though of course she would clean after herself.

Alma gave her a sideways look, as if she thought the same thing. When she asked how long she planned to stay, Maddie said, "I'm not sure." As the words came out of her mouth, her heart beat fast.

What was she doing? This wasn't like her. Not at all.

Then she told Alma her name—and immediately cringed. She should've given a fake name. She would make a terrible criminal.

Alma chattered about the snow, driving slowly down a curving driveway. Looking at the trees on each side, the branches bending under the wet snow, Maddie stopped being afraid. Now that she was in a car with the heater roaring and the tip of her nose no longer feeling like it might be in danger of dropping onto her lap, she could view it with wonder, the misery and sorrow and anger that were like poison inside her sliding away.

Was everything going to be okay after all?

Of course not, she answered herself. This was just a reprieve, not a solution. But the question wouldn't go away, still shining brightly in Maddie's mind as the single driveway lane opened up to a horseshoe drive, with a house and a detached garage. Gazing at it, Maddie sucked in her breath.

"Surprised?" Alma asked. "Is it too old-fashioned for

you?"

"It looks like a house out of a Christmas card." Maddie stared at the stone house with the cedar roof shingles. It wasn't too big or too small. It looked...just right for her.

Of course, she wouldn't stay forever. Maybe just until after Christmas to give Kris and her family some breathing room. What would it hurt?

"My son used to think it looked like a place out of a fairy tale." Alma chortled. "That was a long time ago. Next year he's graduating from Marquette University with a law degree."

"It does look like a place where a fairy godmother would appear." Maddie spoke slowly and could hear the dreaminess in her voice.

Alma stopped the car in front of the house. "If you saw one, what would you say to her?"

Maddie turned to Alma. "I think you're the fairy godmother."

"Me?" Alma laughed loudly, her hand over her breastbone. "Oh lord, when I tell Dexter that, he'll laugh so hard his belly will feel like it's on fire."

"Then you'd better have some Pepto Bismol in your house, because you look a lot like one to me. I'll just say thank you, and congratulations on your son's law degree. I'm sure he owes a lot to you and your husband."

"We always believed in him, but he believes in us, too." Beaming, Alma opened her door, and a freezing wind gusted into the SUV's interior. "We'd better get you inside. Did you bring any food with you?"

When Maddie admitted she only had an apple and a

bag of cashews, Alma insisted she take a grocery bag from the back seat, telling her there was a can of tuna for the kitten, and she had enough at home for her and Dexter to last until tomorrow when the roads would be clear. Ignoring Maddie's protests and the two twenty-dollar bills she tried the give her, Alma pressed a button to open the trunk.

It really was like a dream. And Alma really was like a fairy godmother. Who said they had to come with golden hair and a wand?

At the front doorway, while Maddie was dragging her suitcases over the snowy driveway, Alma lifted a key from beneath a rubber mat. When Maddie reached the doorway, Alma was already inside.

Maddie glanced down at the mat, protected from the snow by the overhang and the direction of the wind. On the black rubber background, yellow and pink flowers spelled out four words: Welcome To My Home.

Tears warmed Maddie's eyes. When she'd walked into her apartment after work three days ago to find it emptied of everything that had belonged to Todd—and quite a few of her own belongings, along with the early Christmas gifts she'd bought for him and had hidden in her closet—she'd felt as if she'd reached the bottom of her life. As if all hope and happiness were gone. As if life were bleak and the coming months would be about survival and nothing else.

The only thing that kept her going was that she had no other choice but to put one foot in front of another. To get through one day, and then the next, and then the one after that. All her emotions shut down, because if she allowed herself to feel, she would scream and cry and grab lamps and dishes then throw them on the floor and walk on broken glass and not care that her feet were bleeding.

And what would that help? Not a damn thing.

So this morning she'd packed, taking care not to break anything. She'd taken her secondhand furniture and lamps to the consignment store, giving Todd's recliner to the neighbor who helped her. Then she'd carried her suitcases to her car, shutting down her emotions and locking them away.

And now...still standing on the doorway as the icy bullets changed to large flakes, she let go of a suitcase handle and put her hand over her still-flat stomach.

"This is a sign, baby," she murmured softly. "I think everything is going to be okay."

She inhaled deeply, her diaphragm opening wide for the first time in a week. Exhaling, she stepped into the hall, dragging her suitcases with her. She reminded herself that this wasn't permanent...and it wasn't hers.

And any good she had here was going to turn sour unless she paid it forward.

2

Five years later...

A car chased Dog. He ran and ran and ran. Someone threw food at him, trying to make him turn and come to the car. Trying to make him stay.

Hunger burned a hole in Dog's belly. He wanted badly to stay, badly to eat.

But there was another hole inside him, in his chest, cold and frozen. The way he'd felt when he was taken away from his mom and brothers and sisters and kept in a cage in the back of a house where the people were hardly there.

Until he'd finally broken out, the wire cutting his leg. But he hadn't let it stop him. With blood dripping down his leg, he'd run. And he'd run and run and run.

This was another day, and he was in a city now, still running. He didn't know these people, the smells and voices unfamiliar as the man stuck his head out of the window and yelled that he had food for Dog. Lots of food.

Dog knew what food meant. He knew what a lot of things meant. More than other dogs, he suspected, but he didn't know for sure, having been away from his brothers and sister since he was a puppy.

The food the man held out the window smelled good, but he didn't like the scents of the people in the car. They smelled like the people who'd taken him into their home and locked him in a cage. And something else was wrong with their smells. Blood. That's what he smelled. Blood and death.

Though his stomach wanted food, he ran faster. Changing directions, he ran through yards, leaving the car behind. The scent of water came to his nose, and he veered toward it. Finally he reached a big body of water. He ducked his head to it, drinking the cold water until he couldn't drink anymore, his belly full of water, his hunger eased just a little. Then he peed all around him to let other animals know this was his territory. That he was there. Only then did he lie down and nap.

When he woke up, night was coming, the light going down. After he drank more water, he lifted his head and sniffed something good. Something wonderful. He ran away from the lake, the smell getting stronger until he reached a garbage can.

There. He stared at the garbage can that was blending into the dusk. It had a cover on it. How was he supposed to get the top off?

He stepped back and back and back. And then he ran forward, full speed. Jumping up, he knocked it over with his front feet. It clattered to the grass, the cover popping off, stuff spilling out of it.

Food! He had food!

He ate and ate and ate, telling himself he was a very smart dog. He had always thought so, but now he knew.

When he was done, he headed back to the water. Drank more and left. As he ran, he realized it was getting colder. He should turn around and go back to a place where it was warmer. He didn't like it when the air was too hot. But he didn't like it when it was too cold, either.

But something was drawing him forward, something in the air. He lifted his head, and the very faint smell of a human came to him.

The right human.

His heart thumped. So did his tail.

It was *his* human. The one he'd been looking for since...forever. Even before he'd left his mom and brothers and sisters.

He didn't know how he knew this, but he'd known this since before he was even born. As if it came from another lifetime.

***

"You're Ruth's grandson!" A sixtyish woman with a figure that reminded Logan MacLeesh of a barrel parked her shopping cart next to him in the Angel Lake Grocery Mart cereal aisle and gazed up at him. Way up. "I haven't seen you for a long time. Decades. You must've been a young teen then, but you have Ruth's eyes. Even in her eighties, she had those bright blue eyes. Laser blue, my daughter calls it. I'm right, aren't I? Are you going to her house?"

Though he nodded, he gave her the bored, haughty look he'd cultivated for paparazzi. The caretakers for his grandmother's house were the only ones in this small town who knew about his visit. He'd called his lawyer over an hour ago. The caretakers must have spread the word already.

"I'm so glad for this chance to thank you." Her voice throbbed with emotion. "I don't know what my Sarah would've done without your help."

"I'm sorry." He drew his head back. "I don't believe I know your Sarah."

She sniffed, and two tears traveled down her chubby cheeks. "Maddie said you'd say that. She said you hated thanks."

"Maddie was right." Whoever the hell she was.

"Maddie's always right." She patted his arm, and she had the fervent look in her eyes that made him brace himself for a quick escape. "I just wanted to let you know that Sarah is fine now. She's working as a nurse in Oshkosh, and she has a new boyfriend who treats her like a princess. But without your refuge, I don't know what would've happened to her."

His refuge?

"My grandmother's house?"

"You're a wonderful man. I'll tell Sarah. She'll be thrilled that I've seen you." She patted his arm again. "I'll tell her how handsome you are." She giggled like a young girl. "You look just like Paul Newman when he was young, only with dark hair. He was always my favorite."

He cocked an eyebrow and was about to ask her if she was flirting with him, but that would lead to laughter and conversation and perhaps getting to know his grandmother's neighbors. None of which he wanted. Instead, he thanked her coolly, grabbed a box of gluten-free cereal with nuts and dried berries and honey, and dropped it into his shopping cart.

She backed up like he was royalty. He nodded at her and headed the other way, toward the two cash registers, hoping he wouldn't run into her again and thinking he needed to call his lawyer to get the name of the people taking care of his house.

At the end of the aisle, a young, gaunt-faced man waited for him, a nervous tic making his eye jump.

"Um, I heard the owner of Ruth MacLeesh's home was in town. It's you, isn't it?" Without waiting for a reply, he rushed on, "It has to be. No one else would stop off to buy groceries. Maybe summer when the lake is open, but not this time of year. I know Maddie gave you our thanks, but I wanted to thank you in person, for letting us stay in your house after the fire. Without your help, I don't know what we would've done."

"I didn't do anything," Logan said. He judged the man to be about thirty. Only three years younger than he was, but in life's experience, about twenty years younger.

"You did *everything*." Moisture filled the man's eyes. "Maybe it meant nothing to you, but without you... I just don't know what we would've done, what with the doctor bills and everything else. You saved us, you did."

Shit. This was worse than the paparazzi. At least he could sneer at them and turn his back, avoiding most of the exposure. After all, he wasn't their prey; it was always the woman on his arm.

The woman who was on someone else's arm now.

He muttered that he was glad everything was better with his family then put his head down and wheeled the cart to the cash register at a quick pace.

At last, he was at the checkout, manned by a woman his age with a robotic face and no smile who kept gazing at the store's exit, obviously wishing she were anywhere else besides this rinky-dink grocery store.

Then she took a good look at him, and her face lit up.

"It's you," she whispered. "It has to be you. You look just like I thought you did."

"Stop." He held up his hand. He didn't know what was going on and didn't want to know. "Whatever you do, don't thank me."

Her chin wobbled; her eyes filled. "Maddie warned me you wouldn't want thanks." She sniffed then proceeded to check out his cereal and a half dozen other items efficiently. His neck prickled. He felt stares on his back as he pulled out his credit card.

"I'm not letting you pay," she said. "It's the least I can do to repay you."

"No, I'll do it."

"I wish you'd let me do it. I owe it to you."

"Pay for someone else's groceries. Someone who needs it." He couldn't believe he'd said the sappy words. He swiped his card and listened to her fervent avowal that she knew just the person she could help.

And she would tell her it was all due to him.

He closed his mouth to hold back a groan.

Two minutes later, he was in his rental car and hoped it didn't look like he was fleeing.

What had just happened here?

Someone had leaked that he was coming, and it had to be the caretakers. And what the hell had all that thank-you crap meant?

He'd come to his grandmother's old home in cold-as-a-freezer Wisconsin for one thing: to be left alone. No paparazzi, no drama, no interruptions.

No women.

16

The always-calm female voice of the GPS on his cell phone told him his destination was on the left in one hundred feet. He turned onto a curving driveway and recalled a few memories of his grandmother. She'd played with him and kissed him and made him laugh. So different from his Anglophile parents, who'd treated him like a small adult and tried to instill in him their own passions.

The last time he'd seen his grandmother, he was only thirteen, already taller than her. She'd made him smile, especially the way she teased his dad, her son, who took it so painfully. His dad wasn't a man who liked to be teased. When they'd left, his grandmother had hugged and kissed him good-bye, and he remembered feeling embarrassed.

That was twenty years ago. She'd been dead for about nine years now. He could've visited her but hadn't. He was pretty sure his father hadn't left his beloved England to visit her, either. Not even to come to her funeral.

His hands tightened on the steering wheel, and he forced himself to loosen his grip. He hadn't expected to feel anything for his grandmother but a mild affection, a mild remembrance. After all, he hadn't really known her.

But that love... It was hard to forget feeling so loved....

The driveway straightened, and he could see the house, like a fairy-tale cottage from the English countryside at Christmastime, though Christmas was still a month and a half away. And since this was Wisconsin, a carpet of snow blanketed the grass.

Only one thing was out of place: the SUV in front of the house with the rear door open and boxes and a suitcase inside it.

He parked behind it, got out of his car...and smiled.

He'd had a few crappy months, and he was in the mood to eviscerate someone.

3

Ginger's plaintive meow warned Maddie that something was wrong. She stopped her frantic packing and heard the door open then close.

Every muscle in her body tensed.

It wasn't Alma or Dexter. They would call before they came. And even then, they'd ring the doorbell. They wouldn't just walk right in. After five years, they considered it her house, though Maddie always remembered she was a liar and a lawbreaker.

She was almost glad it was at an end. She'd been ready to leave so often—and then someone else would need a temporary home. Her way to pay it forward for her lucky break.

And now her luck had run out. Her last guests, Cindy and her baby, had left two months ago to stay with Cindy's mother-in-law in Atlanta. The only other person staying with her was Zach—also known as the best boy in the world.

Most of the time.

And the smartest boy in the world.

Most of the time.

And the boy she loved more than any other in the world.

All of the time.

Zach was in his kindergarten classroom with the other four-year-olds, so it couldn't be him.

Her heart pounded. It had to be *him*. The mysterious

owner. Alma had called her less than an hour ago to tell her the owner was on his way. That's all the lawyers had told her; they hadn't given her any specific time or even a general time.

For all Maddie knew, "on the way" might have meant a day away.

Or ten minutes away.

So she'd left work and sped to the place she'd claimed as her own for the last five years.

She straightened her shoulders now. Maybe whoever it was wouldn't charge her with anything. The neighbors thought the late owner's professor son had inherited it. Maybe he would be a kindly older man—a philanthropist—who would find her story humorous. Or touching. Who would admire her for the help she'd given to other people. Who would appreciate the way she'd fixed up the place.

Or would consider her a thief, a cheat, and a squatter.

Her head held high, she strode out of her bedroom then down the hall to the living room.

A man was taking off a leather jacket, exposing a tallish, slender frame except for his wide shoulders, his back to her, hanging the jacket on the coat rack by the front door. About five eleven, he wasn't bad to look at from the backside. Then he turned, and her breath sucked in, and it felt as if someone had kicked her in the stomach.

Maybe because this mattered so much, a pivotal moment in her life and her son's life, time slowed, and the seconds dragged out to moments, the details imprinting in her brain. His eyes, flame-blue and deep-set. Her gaze clung to his, yet she noted the shadows under his cheekbones, his full mouth, and the clean lines of his jaw. His black hair shot with premature gray belied his skin, firm and unlined. An anomaly.

She suspected this man had many anomalies.

Her second suspicion was that a man that good-looking wouldn't be as sympathetic to her plight as an ugly one.

Why oh why couldn't he have been deformed and ugly?

Squaring her shoulders, she took a deep breath and headed toward him with a wide smile and her hand out, as if she were sent here as the town's official greeter. "Hi! It's nice to meet you. I'm Maddie Barrymore." She may as well tell him her real name. He could easily find out what it was.

His eyebrows rose, but he shook her hand. "Related to the acting Barrymores?"

"Not that I know, though my stepmother claims we connect somewhere."

"As in the wicked stepmother?"

"Not really. I wish she and my dad lived nearby, but my dad is stationed in Alaska. You're Mr. MacLeesh, aren't you?"

"Logan MacLeesh. Are you going to ask me for identification?"

"Yes." She was taking a chance here, but she'd taken a chance every day she'd lived in his house. She'd never thought of herself as a risk taker, but she'd lived as one for five years already, so perhaps she was fooling herself.

The look he gave her now was amused. No question

about it. He slid his wallet out of his back pocket and took out something, stepping closer to hand it to her.

She grasped the plastic card and saw it was a California driver's license. Even his driver's license picture looked good. Nothing like hers, which could be used as a "don't" image for photographers. From his birth date, she saw he was thirty-three, only six years older than her.

Not that the age difference mattered.

Or that there was no ring on his left hand.

She handed the license back to him. "Would you like me to take you on a tour of the place?"

"*My* place?"

She kept the polite smile on her face. "Yes."

"My lawyer told me the caretakers were an older couple. Did they ask you to show it to me?"

Her smile dipped. He wasn't falling for her show of confidence. He knew. Damn it, he knew.

"No, they have nothing to do with my presence here."

He nodded, not taking his eyes off her, pursing his lips—especially the full lower lip—as if considering what to do with her.

She knew what she needed to do. Bluff him into letting her go without punishing anyone else. Already she held her head higher, a gesture of poise instead of worry, her smile fixed in place. The one that said I-like-you-and-I-know-you-like-me-too.

"So, you realize I've been living here?" she asked.

"You mean squatting." His striking blue eyes roamed down her body, very slowly, then up again. Like she was a piece of meat.

She hated it. Yet her body didn't hate it, her skin prickling, hormones waking up after a long sleep.

"What are you thinking?" he asked.

"You wouldn't believe me."

"Try me."

"I know what I've done was—"

A meow cut through her words, and paws padded into the living room from the back bedroom. The next second, Ginger stood in front of her, meowing at him, a whole string of meows and mewls and mrrrooos. Each with its own inflection and tone.

He waited until Ginger was done before jerking his gaze up to Maddie. "I get the feeling your cat is telling me off."

"Oh? You have a guilty conscience?"

His cynical half smile came back. "Do you?"

"You want the whole story?" She gestured behind her. "It's not short. Would you like to hear it in the kitchen? With coffee or tea? Or cocoa? I have pumpkin bread."

His lips twitched, his blue eyes glinting, all the signs of held-back laughter.

Her tension eased, and she gave him a tentative smile.

"You're something," he said.

She suspected that might not be a compliment but said, "I've always thought everyone is something."

"Coffee sounds about right to me." He gestured to her to go ahead of him.

Without saying a word, she headed to the kitchen. At the first step, she thought of emphasizing the movement of her hips instead of her usual straight-forward, get-me-to-where-I-need-to-go stride. But she didn't think a little jiggle would impress this man, and it would just embarrass her.

"You live here alone?" he asked as they entered the open kitchen. "Besides the cat?"

"I have a son."

"How old?"

"Four years, six months."

"How long have you lived here?"

She took down a mug for him. Hers was already on the counter. "Five years."

His eyebrows rose. "So you were three months pregnant when you moved in."

That was a mild reaction to her admission. She didn't know what to make of him. Didn't know if it was a good thing or not. "You're good at math. It's nothing to do with Alma and Dexter."

He looked blankly at her.

"Dexter Young is your caretaker," she said. "Alma's his wife. I gave them the impression I was here with your permission."

"Why?"

"I was broke and pregnant. That's the short explanation."

He stared at her, unresponsive. She turned to the counter, her back to him. Last Christmas, she'd splurged on one of the pour-one-cup-with-a-push-of-a-button coffeemakers, and now she wished she would've saved the money—even though it'd been on sale—because if this didn't go right, she'd need every penny she could scrounge up to pay a lawyer.

She brought two mugs of coffee to the round kitchen table first then cut two thick slices of pumpkin bread with walnut and pineapple, one for him and one for herself. She took the chair across the table from where he stood. If she dined and drank coffee with him, it might make him reluctant to charge her with anything.

"I had a long drive," he said, sitting with his legs apart, "and I'm hungry. Otherwise I wouldn't be breaking bread with you."

A shiver quivered through her. He knew all the angles.

He ate the pumpkin bread quickly, his eyebrows going up again. Only then did he take a sip of coffee. He looked down at her slice of pumpkin bread.

She slid it across to him. "I've lost my appetite."

"I'm not letting you off the hook for two slices of pumpkin bread, no matter how good it is. What about your son's father? Does he have anything to do with this?"

"The day after I told him about the pregnancy, I came home from work and he was gone." She grimaced. "Along with my GPS and everything else I had of value."

He looked at her, unblinking, not saying anything.

She put her hand around the mug. The warmth calmed her nerves a bit. "My sister and brother-in-law live with their two kids in Eagleton. It was just one then. I was going to stay with them until I saved enough money to get my own place. Driving to their place, I got stuck in your driveway during a blizzard. Don't ask me how." She glared at him, though glaring probably wasn't the smart way to handle it.

Be charming, she told herself. Pretend you're a nice person who only did what you did because you had no choice.

But she couldn't say that. There were always choices.

She wasn't even going to mention Ginger running in front of the car. It would sound manipulative, as if she were using her cat to soften him up. Especially to this man. He had a look of a cynic, a man who'd seen the dark side of life. And if he saw the bright side, he'd keep looking until he saw the speck of tarnish.

She couldn't deny that her specks were easy to find.

"Then Alma stopped to help me," she continued. "Because I was on your driveway, she thought I was going to stay here. And I, uh, well..." She made a face. "I let her think that."

"She gave you the idea?"

Maddie jerked her head up. "No! Alma had nothing to do with it. When I was a child, I was captivated by the *Puss in Boots* story. If anything gave me the idea, that's it."

He brought up his hand and scratched the cleft in his chin, his eyes narrowed, and he rubbed his chin slowly.

She picked up her coffee and swallowed, needing the caffeine energy boost.

"Sounds like you know a lot of stories." His wry voice told her he wasn't giving her a compliment.

"I'm my son's official storyteller." She pushed loose strands of hair behind her ear. His gaze followed her movement. Her face warmed, and she spoke quickly. "I was going to just stay until after Christmas, but then my sister was having problems with her pregnancy. There were a few bad months for her. Having me in their small house would've been hard on them."

"And after that?"

"By the time the baby was born, I got a job at...well, in town."

"Where in town?"

Her face heated. "The town hall."

His lips twitched once then straightened to a line. "You work at the town hall?"

"Yes. I already had three years of college, and I could type. My former employer gave me a good reference. And by then..."

"By then what?"

"Nothing." She shook her head. By then she'd had her first temporary guest—a local woman whose boyfriend had kicked her out of their house and moved in his new girlfriend.

He looked at her for a long moment, and it felt to her as if he *knew*, though that was impossible. "Show me the rest of the house," he said, getting to his feet.

She stood, feeling numb. At least he wasn't calling the sheriff yet. If he did that, everything she'd worked for would fall apart, even more than it had already. The town board would fire her. How could they trust her? And it would be hard to get another one. Who would want to hire a squatter?

She started with the former sewing room in the back, converted into a bedroom for Zach, and across the hall, the bigger bedroom for herself. He peered at the half-packed suitcase without saying a word before heading to the stairway, taking the lead.

Upstairs, he looked at the big bedroom with the queen-sized bed and asked her if that's where the others had stayed.

Her breath sucked in again, and she stepped away from him then made herself stand still. "You know?"

"When I stopped at the local grocery store, I was accosted by three people who thanked me."

"This is going to sound corny, but when I first stayed here, I promised myself that, if I could, I'd help other people in need."

"By letting them stay in my house? Without my permission?"

"I shouldn't have done it. I know it." She looked straight into his eyes. "But the house was empty for years. As far as I knew, the real owner had forgotten about it. And...and..." She raised her hands then dropped them.

He just stared at her. She wanted to wrap her arms across her chest, as if to protect herself from his eyes that saw too much. But she didn't. The gesture would tell him she was nervous, that she was hiding herself from him.

"Why didn't you stay upstairs?" He gestured at the bedroom. "It's much bigger."

She paused. Would he believe her? Well, since he was standing in front of her, waiting, she had no other choice but to answer truthfully.

"I thought if I stayed in the smaller rooms, I'd be taking less advantage of you." She bit her lower lip then realized what she was doing and released it. "I have no excuse for what I've done, but I can pay you rent for the five years I've lived here. I know what it costs to rent a home in the town, and as soon as I got my job, I set up a separate bank account. Every month, I've been depositing money to pay the owners."

He continued to stare at her, and she put her weight on one foot then the other. His lips were curved up, but it was a cold smile, and his eyes were still narrowed, as if he was thinking of a way to punish her. She could read it in his face. His very handsome face.

It was a good thing she didn't go for handsome men anymore. "I can go to the bank with you right now and pay you with cash. Or I can write you a check. Or...or..."

"I have an idea," he said then headed downstairs, letting her follow him or not. Letting her take her sweet time, as if she really had a choice.

She headed downstairs after him.

4

Logan didn't know why he was doing this. Amusement? Pity? At least she hadn't blamed anyone but herself. Maybe that was her plan. Be the brave little soldier girl. So much more sympathetic and likable than if she cried and whined.

"I can just leave," she said, a nervous edge in her voice. "Give you the money and go."

He didn't answer her, gazing at the living room. Despite the cottage look on the outside, the living room was open to the kitchen, giving it a modern feel. He took in the light gray walls and the aqua sofa with orange pillows. Modern mixed with traditional. His grandmother's furniture had been heavier and fussier. "It looks different."

"I painted and changed the furniture. It was, um..."

"Ugly," he finished.

"Not my taste," she said firmly. "The old furniture is in the attic and the basement. I didn't touch the upstairs, except to clean and change the bedding. I can easily take my stuff out and return it to the way it was."

"No. Leave it."

She sucked in her lips between her teeth then quickly released them and frowned at him instead.

What the hell was he going to do with her? Charge her? Call the cops? Kick her ass to the curb? Let her work off the rent?

He'd come here to be alone, but being alone hadn't

worked for him for the last three months. Not in California. Not in New York. Not in Italy. Not in Greece.

But in the few minutes he was in the house, she'd entertained him. Listening to her, he'd felt...curious. A couple times, he'd even felt on the verge of laughter.

"You know who I am?" he asked.

Her forehead creased. "Are you an actor? You look familiar."

He screwed up his lips. "I'm a...writer. And director. And producer."

"What did you write?"

"Never mind." He hadn't called himself a writer for years and didn't know why he'd mentioned it. "It was long ago and far away."

She nodded, not asking any other questions. He narrowed his eyes. "You're going to leave it like that?" he asked, not believing she'd do that. No woman he knew would leave it.

"Sure. I can Google you later."

He laughed, and he realized that this was his first real laugh in the last three months. And the gray fog that had wrapped around him since he'd left California had—

"Why are you staring at me?" she asked.

Thinned, he thought. The fog had thinned.

"You amuse me. I have an idea..."

She sat up straight, invisible prickles shooting off her skin. He could practically see the cynicism in her eyes. The knowledge that men usually did have an idea, and it often involved nudity.

"Nothing like that," he said.

"Like what?" She frowned suspiciously.

"Kinky."

Her cheeks flushed a deep vermillion.

"You don't have to worry about me making unwanted advances. Would you believe me if I said I was under the spell of a dark queen?" He smiled as he spoke, but there was no smile inside him. Just the blackness. "That she stole my heart, and unless she's nearby, I'm heartless?"

"Heartless? Does that mean..." She lowered her gaze to below his belt and winced. "Never mind."

He held back a grimace. For a woman who seemed so proper, she was clearly having improper thoughts. He was almost tempted to tell her that his dick operated just fine, so he could see her face turn the color of the inside of a ripe watermelon.

As if she read his mind, her eyes shot up, questions still in their depths. Hazel eyes, with brown surrounded by green that was surrounded by dusky blue, and not medium brown, as he'd first thought. Everything about her was like that. His first impression had been of an ordinary woman. Attractive but not stunning. Medium height, medium weight. Brown hair with a bit of red and a bit of a wave, falling just below her shoulders. Practical but silky. There was quietude to her but enough spunk that she didn't fade into the background.

And she wasn't the scheming opportunist he'd thought she was when he'd come into the house and she'd walked toward him with the fake smile.

And there was one more thing. Nothing about her screamed sex...but from the first sentence she'd spoken to him, the first touch of their hands, he'd felt the whisper of the attraction, drawing her to him like a starving dog to a steak.

This was a bad idea.

But what did he have to lose? If it didn't work out, he could pack up and leave.

He'd make sure she and her son left, too.

"I started off as a writer," he said. "I wrote one screenplay when I was twenty-two. No one wanted to make it into a movie, so I did it myself."

"Does the movie have a title?"

"You'll find out when you Google me."

"So I will." She crossed her legs then uncrossed them. She was wearing practical black slacks, but he suspected her legs might be spectacular.

"It took three years of my life to find backers, put it together, and find distributors. In the end, it turned out to be a breakout hit," he said. "After that, I was asked by...an actress who admired my work to produce and direct a movie for her."

He fell silent. Olivia had been the actress. He'd been immediately enamored. She was like no one he'd ever met before. So vivid, so alive. Magical and mesmerizing. One journalist had said she sucked up all the air in the room, commanding the room's attention, like the brightest star in the sky at night. Of all the comments written about her, that was the truest.

"What other movies did you write?" Maddie asked, commanding his attention.

"None." He spoke without inflection, as if it didn't matter. "The stories dried up."

"Dried up? Like a well?"

Like my soul, he thought. The juice of life squeezed

out of it, leaving a shell of himself. "Call it whatever you want. My well is dry, and it needs to be replenished."

Her eyebrows contracted. "I don't know what you mean."

"The screenplay I wrote that brought me to L.A. mattered to me. Not because it was brilliant or life changing, but because it was *mine*." As he talked to her, he was talking to himself, too. All this was in his gut, part of his tangled emotions. Now he was untangling them out loud to both of them. "Everything I did later was something other people believed in. I helped make their dreams come true. Now it's time for me to go back to my dreams and…"

"And do what?" She leaned toward him.

"Do you know anything about the Muses?"

"You're testing my knowledge about Greek mythology? My major was in business, not myths. All I remember is that they're daughters of some god, and a muse is supposed to inspire people."

"That's right. I need a muse, and I think you're it."

"Me?" Her voice squeaked.

"You." He could see the doubt in her face, could practically read the questions racing through her mind. "In this short time we've been talking, I've already gotten a spark of an idea. The first in a long time. I don't know if I'll use it, but it's a start."

"And you think it's from something I said?"

"I know it is. I'll make you a deal. You and your son can stay here, but you have to tell me a story every night."

"A story? What makes you think I have any stories to

tell?"

"You said you're your son's storyteller. And in this short time, you've been telling me a lot of stories. You've...amused me."

"Should I be flattered?"

"In your case, you should be grateful."

Instead of looking at him thankfully, her lips flattened, and her eyes narrowed.

He fought an urge to laugh. "Tell me one story a night, and you and your son can stay until I leave."

"Like the woman in *The Arabian Nights*? Telling the Persian king a story every night?"

"One thousand and one nights." He lowered his voice, purposely making it seductive, and she jerked back. "Just a story. Nothing else. Are you up to it? Or would you rather pack up and leave?" He paused then added, "Go ahead, I won't call the sheriff on you. I won't charge you for the years you lived here. You're free to leave with no consequences."

"You're serious?"

"About leaving?"

"About not making me pay you anything?"

"That's what matters most to you?"

She lowered her gaze, frowning, and her hands curled into fists.

He gave her time to think. The money didn't mean anything to him, but he'd been a broke college student. And then he'd been broke for years after that while making his movie. He knew what it was like to eat Ramen noodles for dinner night after night. If she'd put sixty months' worth of rent in a bank account, she probably had enough for a down payment on a house. What meant nothing to him might mean everything to her.

She sat straight, no longer leaning back. "That's a very strange suggestion. I have my son to consider."

"It's not your son you'd have to worry about around me."

Her eyes shot up. "Are you saying *I'd* have to worry?"

"Not really." The blackness was creeping up on him again. It was in his voice. Dragging and dull. "I like women, not children, but I've never forced myself on one. And you can leave anytime."

"Before the one thousand one nights are up?"

"Anytime."

"Now?"

He closed his eyes. The blackness was filling up all the spaces in him. Crowding around his bones, his organs, his heart. "Go. Right now. Pack up. Leave."

A creak came, the sound of her getting to her feet. She touched his arm, and he slowly opened his eyes to see her frowning at him in concern.

"Are you okay?"

"I'm fine. You can go."

She took a deep breath. "If you really mean it, I'll stay. At least for now. I might not have any stories. You might hate them. I might hate telling them. The main thing is that Zach is okay."

He shrugged, even as he realized her answer had mattered to him. If she'd said no, he would've been disappointed.

"I'll have to get back to work for now." She took two

steps then stopped and looked back. "I'm making chicken for dinner tonight. If you'd like to join Zach and me, I'll have enough for you." Not waiting for his answer, she strode away, purpose in every step.

Watching her leave, he felt...different, more alive. The blackness shrank away from his bones, his organs, his heart. Letting in a thin beam of light. The feeling was so foreign he was tempted to push the light away.

But he didn't. He doubted it would stay. Though he'd enjoyed this exchange of dialogue with Maddie, this was a pale shadow of the way he felt whenever he saw Olivia, his dark queen. With her, he'd been more alive than he'd ever been before or since. She'd sent fire flaming through his veins. It hadn't been comfortable, and it hadn't been pleasant, but with her, every sense had expanded. He hadn't needed food, he hadn't needed drink, he'd just needed her.

Olivia had been his morphine. Since she'd left his life, not looking back, every day had been a gray day.

The most beautiful women in Hollywood and New York hadn't been able to change that. Not even a glimmer of light.

He didn't expect this average woman in this small Wisconsin town to change that. At the least, she could distract him for a short time. And at the most, she might amuse him.

5

Five hours later, the kitchen smelled of roast chicken, and Maddie was introducing her son to him. As she did, he could practically see invisible armor spring up on her, hear the clank of metal, see an invisible lance in her hand. She reminded Logan of a small gladiator, ready to take down the dragon if he breathed even a small plume of fire.

The boy resembled his mother, but his eyes were pure green instead of hazel. He had her direct stare, looking him straight in the eyes, his shoulders squared. In his own way, ready for a blast of dragon fire.

"Are you going to live with us?" Zach Barrymore asked.

Logan looked at Maddie, with one eyebrow up. She had moved to the counter and was spooning roasted vegetables onto a platter. Let her make the explanations to her son.

"Zach, you know we don't own this house. Mr. MacLeesh is the real owner. He's going to stay upstairs, and we're going to stay downstairs."

A frown marred Zach's clear forehead, and he kept his gaze on Logan. "Does this mean you're my mom's boyfriend?"

Maddie groaned, setting down the serving spoon. "Zach! You're being rude. I told you—"

"Mom, Mark's mom told him the same thing about her boyfriend. And now she's got a baby in her tummy, and he bosses Mark around. I don't want this man bossing me around."

Ginger, the orange and white cat, sat on the floor by the back hall and stared at Logan with unblinking eyes. Logan was sure she agreed with the boy.

"As long as you don't touch any of my stuff," Logan said, "I won't tell you what to do."

"Then you have to not touch my stuff."

"Zach!"

Humor spiked inside Logan. Before today, he'd gone weeks without anything to smile or laugh at. It felt...odd.

"It's fine," he said, keeping his gaze on the boy. "I understand exactly how Zach feels, and I appreciate his courage in telling me." He lowered his head toward the boy. "You're a dragon slayer, you know that?"

Zach's eyes widened. "If I see a dragon, I'll take my mom's biggest knife." He raised his hands over his right shoulder. "And wait until he's sleeping—"

"Good strategy," Logan said.

"I know. Then I'll climb up on his body and bring the sword down on it." He bent forward, smashing down his invisible sword. "Blood will squirt out all over, and the dragon will shake all over, and it will scream. Like this." He opened his mouth, and a howl more suited to a wolf than a dragon came out, though Logan admitted he didn't know what a dragon's roar would sound like.

The cat yowled and dashed out of the kitchen.

"Zach, don't scare Ginger." Maddie headed toward the table, carrying the platter of cut-up chicken. "And you better not take any of my knives to kill anything, or I'll have to take away your game playing time."

"Mom, what if a dragon is hiding in the house?"

"Then yell at it and use your Ninja moves, okay?"

The boy stared at her, his eyebrows contracted, obviously thinking this through. "Okay," he finally said. "I'll scare it with my Ninja fighting moves."

"Good boy." She set the platter on the table. "Mr. MacLeesh isn't my boyfriend. He's the owner of this house. The real one."

Zach's forehead still puckered. "Mommy, this is our home. I don't want to move to a new place."

"Honey, it doesn't matter where we live. As long as we have each other, we'll be happy."

"But I like this house." His voice rose.

"I like it, too. And we're not moving now. But if we do, I'll find a house that we both like." She stared down at him, radiating calmness. "Okay?"

"And Ginger?" he asked.

"And Ginger."

He gave her a long look, as if waiting for her to back down, but that wasn't happening. He sighed heavily, his shoulders drooped, and he nodded. She bent forward, and though she spoke in a low tone, her voice traveled. "Love you, my brave dragon slayer."

He swept his hands around his mother's thighs, his head against her hip. "Mommy, I won't let any dragon kill you. Not never."

She kissed the top of his head, hugging him back. Then she straightened, and he unhooked his arms from her. The tender moment over, she handed him sautéed vegetables and potatoes to take to the table, telling him he should thank Logan for letting him live there.

The boy frowned as he obeyed his mother, still obviously unsure whether to trust him or not. Logan admired his suspicion. Not yet five and the boy didn't believe everything the adults said. Smart boy. In show business as in life, it was wise to doubt and smarter to distrust. Logan knew about it. Show business was just a microcosm of every area of life, where promises were broken faster than a blink, and with about the same amount of warning.

Hearts could be broken that fast, too.

Broken, smashed, stepped on, and tossed away.

Right now, the heart beating in his chest was only good for pushing blood through it. Nothing else. He could appreciate love—especially the love between a mother and her son—but was numb to the emotion himself. It left him an observer of life instead of a participant. The thought gave him a measure of peace, and he felt a stirring in him. A sense of tranquility.

Maybe this was the best thing that had happened to him.

***

The shed door was open, and the dog crept in. He'd wanted to stay out in the open on the grass. But other animals could find him there. The predators. He was in a place with few homes and more trees. He'd seen animal waste that did not come from a small animal, and he'd smelled something he'd never smelled before.

But he'd also smelled a tiny whiff of the familiar scent—the human scent that told him *home*. His home.

He remembered dreaming of that home when he was in his mother's belly. And when he was drinking milk from her. Knowing that his human would find him.

But it hadn't happened. Instead, the other humans had found him.

He lay down in a corner of the shed. It was still cold here but not so cold that his legs felt numb. The air wasn't as fresh as outside, but it was better than the smell in his cage where he'd lived before this. Where some days his water wasn't changed, and it would run out. And some days, they didn't clean his waste. And then they yelled at him.

Those days were gone, and he was never going back.

No other animal was in the shed. He smelled that mice used to live there, but it was a long-time-ago scent.

He laid his head down, trusting that any suspicious noises or smells would wake him, and he fell asleep.

No dreams came, but the scent of his human entered his brain, and a spark went off, connecting with another spark, and another, and another, and so on and so on.

And spark by spark, as he slipped into heavy sleep, his subconscious awoke....

***

Maddie watched Logan from the hall. Sitting back on the recliner, his legs up, he oozed sex, reminding her of a jaded hero in a romance book.

Taking a deep breath, she stepped into the living room.

"Your son's asleep?" Logan asked. Ginger jumped on

his lap, and he petted her slowly with his long, slender fingers. Ginger purred, and her front paws kneaded his thigh.

Maddie nodded. The living room area was warmer than Zach's bedroom, and she saw that he'd lit the fire in the fireplace. Too warm outside for her to burn wood this early, though it was supposed to reach freezing later on tonight. But freezing was nothing to her when she was inside her house with the furnace humming. *His* house, she reminded herself. A distasteful thought but the truth. It was also true that locals only called it really cold when it was below zero, with wind chills lower than that.

As George, the town administrator, liked to say on his biweekly office appearance, "Cold enough to freeze off a man's balls."

And every time he left the room after saying it, Caroline, the deputy clerk, a thin, redheaded woman in her late fifties, would say, "I wish it would freeze off *his* balls."

Maddie set down her glass of wine and sat on the couch across from the recliner. She tried not to look at his caressing fingers on Ginger's back, but the movement was mesmerizing.

A small ache started low in her belly. It had been so long since any man had touched her like that. Her choice. Plenty of men had given her signals that they wanted her. She'd turned down and discouraged more offers than she could remember. A few times, she'd been tempted, but she had her reasons to refuse.

She forced her gaze from his hands to his face. His lips curved up, as if he read her thoughts and her emotions—and her body temperature, too, aware that it had gone up a couple of degrees.

"Ready for your first story?" she asked.

"It's dark and cold outside. The perfect night for a story."

"Anything specific? A subject you prefer?"

"My only stipulation is that it entertains me."

"What if I'm boring?"

"Then it will be my fault for overestimating you."

Maybe he said that, but she didn't believe it. To her, it was a challenge to make sure she entertained him—and with all her clothes on.

Ginger meowed in what Maddie recognized as a complaint, and she saw his fingers had stilled on the cat's neck. Voicing another complaint, Ginger jumped off his lap then padded over to Maddie.

Maddie took a quick sip of her wine before Ginger leaped up onto her lap then stretched out over her thighs, purring. Waiting for Maddie to do her job.

Someone else who expected something from her. But she was already setting down the glass with one hand and petting her silky-haired, spoiled cat with the other. After five years of cohabitation, she was a well-trained human. As Ginger purred louder, she relaxed.

"I'll tell you about the liar and the maiden," she began. Her tone was different than before, in story mode, with a rhythm she didn't have in her normal speech. "Though to tell the truth, she wasn't quite a maiden. Kind of a dented maiden."

"Dented?" His mouth quirked up.

"Dented," she said firmly. "She'd had a few

encounters, though to tell the truth—again—none of them were that exciting."

"That's often the case."

"You, too?"

"We're talking fiction here, aren't we?"

"Of course." She raised her eyebrows before continuing. "In fact, our heroine began to question the happily-ever-after thing. She was starting to think that maybe love wasn't in the stars for her. So she decided to become a businesswoman instead."

"A wise choice."

"I agree. She came from struggling families, and there was no money for college."

"Families? Plural?"

She swallowed, but her petting never faltered, and she thought she probably looked calm on the outside, though her belly twisted sharply. "Her parents were divorced and remarried and had new families. They lived far away."

"So our heroine had no one?"

"She had a sister, and they lived in a windy city with many other people. She worked part-time and went to the university part-time, and she was buzzing along, living her normal life, eating too many pizzas and drinking too much coffee." She found the happy spot below Ginger's ear, and Ginger purred louder. "Then two things happened."

"She met a man," he said.

"You've heard this story before?"

"Often. It never has a good ending."

"I wouldn't say *never*. Before she met a man, her

45

sister met one."

"Ah. Competitive falling in love."

"I don't think so." She frowned and shook her head, even as she realized the truth. Oh God, he was right. Kris had fallen in love, leaving her alone, and she could remember wishing she was in love, too.

Be careful what you wish for.

But she couldn't think about that now.

"The story?" he said.

"Okay," she said, "the older sister married her boyfriend and moved out of the windy city to a smaller and often colder city. Meanwhile, the other sister, the younger one, was happily dating. And she...well, she thought she fell in love, too."

"Madly?"

"You mean like 'angrily'?" She raised her eyebrows at him as she still petted her cat. "Sometimes. He was a guy, after all."

The corners of his lips lifted, and she felt a lift inside her, too.

"Do you want to hear the story?" She made her tone snotty, knowing it would amuse him. After all, wasn't that the deal? She was his version of a court jester. "Or are you critiquing as I go?"

"Both. I'm the audience. Heckling is a privilege."

"The best comics heckle the heckler right back."

He chuckled. "You can try."

His eyes were bright, and she shifted her attention to her cat. Much safer to gaze at her cat than his face that looked as if God had created him just for her.

Hadn't she learned to avoid handsome men? They

were nothing but trouble. And Todd hadn't been half as handsome as Logan.

"Back to my story. Our heroine—"

"Whose name you never said."

"This is an interactive story. You can name her."

"Princess. Call her Princess."

"I think she hates the name, but, okay, Princess and her boyfriend—let's call him Toad—were getting along wonderfully. He worked as a chef during the day, and she waitressed and went to college. They soon moved in together."

"And were madly in love."

"You keep bringing that up. You have a thing about it?"

"No. In fact, if I thought this did have a happily-ever-after ending with a wedding and kids on the horizon, then I would require you to tell me another story."

"So you only want unhappy stories?"

"Not unhappy. They can be funny or ambiguous or murderous or anything but a man and a woman off to their happily ever after."

"Good to know. I'll work on the list."

"Which does this one fall into?"

"When it's over, you tell me." She took another sip of wine and wished she'd poured herself a bigger glass. Maybe just bring the bottle and chug it down. "Princess wasn't happy that Toad would go out with the guys while she waitressed or studied, but she trusted that he was faithful. And, really, she was more concerned about the money he spent. She was practical. *Very* practical."

"I suppose he was *very* good-looking."

"Well, not as good-looking as *some* men."

"Are you trying to flatter your way out of our deal? It won't work."

"No flattery, just the facts. You have a mirror. You know what your face looks like." She made her voice dry and held herself back from mentioning the rest of his body. That might get her in a different kind of trouble. One she wanted to avoid. "Back to the story. When Toad was home at the same time as Princess, he wanted her to pay attention to him instead of her studies. So she didn't complain when he was away."

"Princess is a rare woman."

"Not really. Quite average, actually. But back to the story again." She narrowed her eyes at him. "The dramatic part is coming."

"Good of you to announce it."

"Zach is a much better audience than you are."

"Go ahead." He waved his hand. "I'm listening. We were at the part where Princess didn't complain about his carousing. What happened next?"

"*It* happened next," she said, and Ginger jumped off her lap with a yowl. Maddie realized she'd stopped petting her. In many ways, the cat was smarter than her. When someone stops giving you attention, walk away. Give one yowl to show your dissatisfaction, then go.

And don't look back.

"What happened?" he asked. "She found out he was unfaithful?"

"That would've been the better scenario." She looked back at him. "She was late."

"Late to work? To class?"

"No. She was *late*."

"Ah. *Late*."

"Yes. Ah. Or, as Toad said, '*Oh shit.*' He asked how it could happen since he used protection all the time, and she said, 'How the hell do you think it happened? Do you think I've been cheating?'"

"The usual conversation."

"Oh, it's happened to you?"

He grinned. "Never. A few friends have been in the same situation—of both sexes—and they've been happy to share their misery."

"In this case, Toad quickly apologized. Made love to her and told her how happy he was. The next day, she went to work, and when she came home he was gone and so were all of his clothes and every item of his. Plus some of hers—including her GPS."

"I believe you mentioned the GPS before."

"If I'd had the GPS, I would've gotten off the expressway at the right exit, and I would never have ended up here." She flapped her fingers at him. "But you're right, I need to let go of my anger over the GPS. And this isn't about me."

"I never once thought it was."

"I'm sure. Anyway, she went to the restaurant where he worked and was told he was offered a job as a chef on a yacht and had taken it."

His face settled in grim lines. "Did she go after him? Force him to claim the child? To support it?"

"She had way too much pride for that. She thought he wasn't a man who deserved her or the child. She never heard from him again."

"So this is the ambiguous ending."

"I have to apologize, because it is the happy ending, at least for our heroine. She has the most wonderful child in the world. So this is *her* happy ending. At least for now." She pushed up from the sofa. "I'm going to bed now. I have to go to work tomorrow. I hope it was satisfactory."

"I found it enlightening."

"I strive to enlighten."

She started past him, and he reached out and wrapped his long fingers around her wrist. "I was wrong about you," he said.

"Wrong about what?" she asked, hoping he wouldn't feel the speeding of her pulse.

"I thought you were ordinary."

"That's the thing; the more you get to know people, the less ordinary they are. In many cases, they'll be extraordinary."

Then she jerked her wrist from his grasp and headed to the bathroom. Her life had changed today, but it didn't change the fact that she'd gotten up early this morning as usual, fed her cat and her son, then drove to work, still yawning. And it didn't change the fact that she had to do the same thing again tomorrow.

And just because the most exciting man she'd ever seen was in her house, breathing the same air as her, it didn't change the fact that after five years of looking at men and thinking, *No, no, no*, her body was suddenly saying, *Yes, yes, yes!*

Life was full of tricks, and it had thrown another big one at her. But Logan hadn't called the sheriff on her, and she hadn't been arrested. And when she said her list of things she was grateful for in her bed that night, that would be one of the top ones.

As she got ready for bed, she wondered one thing: What story would she tell him tomorrow?

***

Dog dreamed of a boy who loved him. Loved him almost as much as he loved the boy back. They ran and played during the daytime. At night, Dog waited until everyone was asleep, and he jumped on the bed to sleep next to the boy. Every day, the boy told Dog how much he loved him. Every school day, long before the boy came home, Dog lay down by the door to wait and wait and wait. And sometimes the boy was doing other things with other people, so Dog had to wait a long, long time.

But when the boy came, Dog was so happy. The boy dropped everything on the floor—even though his mom or dad yelled every time—and he would fall on his knees and they would hug, and Dog would lick the boy's face. He would lick and lick and lick. And the boy would laugh and laugh and laugh.

And then one day...

The dream stopped, and the dog's head jerked up. His heart was pounding, and he was gasping.

It was dark in the shed, so it must still be dark outside. He listened hard for noises but could only hear night sounds from outside. Nothing inside the shed.

Because he'd woken so quickly, he still remembered his dream. Only it didn't feel like a dream. It felt *real*. As if he'd really been there. As if the boy had really been there. As if the love they felt had really happened.

But it hadn't. He remembered everything in his life, and that had never happened.

And at the end, when he'd woken so suddenly...

He knew why. Something bad had been about to happen, and his mind had shut it off.

Dog dropped his head between his paws on the soft ground. Though he closed his eyes, he didn't go to sleep for a long time.

6

L ogan was glad for the snow, glad to shovel it. Glad he was doing something with his day instead of staring at a blank computer screen. Or typing words he'd soon delete.

His first and only screenplay had come in bursts of inspiration, writing in classes and in between classes, scribbling on napkins in restaurants, on backs of bills, on anything he could get his hands on as the words poured out so fast he couldn't keep up with them, writing abbreviated sentences and hoping to hell he'd remember what he'd meant.

Now the words had dried out. Like his heart.

He didn't blame Olivia. He blamed himself.

On his parents' one visit to his ocean-view house, his father had told him that Olivia reminded him of the evil queen in the Disney movies. His father had laughed, as if to take the sting out of his words. But his eyes hadn't laughed; worry had darkened them.

His mother had claimed to like Olivia. But then she'd said it bothered her that Olivia slithered when she walked.

As his mother had said it, she'd laughed, too. But her eyes were as serious as if she'd seen him walk on broken glass.

They didn't understand. Olivia wasn't a witch, and though he was younger than her, she hadn't used witchcraft to enthrall him. In some ways, they were alike.

If he let himself, he could be the male version of her.

Halfway down the front sidewalk, he put down the shovel and looked up at the trees blanketed with new snow, staring until they blurred.

With a little effort, if he really wanted to, he could easily draw Maddie to him.

But there was the son...

He picked up the shovel, braced his legs, and shoveled harder.

Some things he just didn't do.

He had a feeling about this practical woman who'd broken the law by squatting in his house—inspired by a fairy tale, she'd said. A feeling that she'd be good for his stories. As if he were in his own doomed fairy tale, and her stories would help him reclaim his missing soul.

***

Coming down the driveway, Maddie saw the sidewalk was shoveled. Though Dexter plowed the driveway, she always shoveled the sidewalk. Three inches had fallen today, according to the news, but it had been three inches of *wet* snow. And anyone who shoveled wet snow knew it weighed about fifteen times more than fluffy snow.

She'd been up since six thirty this morning, fed breakfast to Zach, took him to school, worked all day, emailed her sister about twenty times, and had a frantic phone call with her about her gorgeous but dangerous landlord, then picked up Zach and his friend Chloe, who always ate with them on Thursdays because her mother worked longer on Thursdays and would pick her up at seven.

By the time she got home, all she wanted to do was conk out for an hour. But of course, that wouldn't happen. Even if she didn't have to shovel, she still had to make dinner.

Logan's rental took up half the garage, and she stopped on the driveway to let Zach and Chloe out. She told them she'd be just a minute, but by the time she parked and hurried out of the garage, they were gone. Logan must have let them inside. One other reason she should be grateful.

Inside the kitchen, Chloe was looking up at Logan with her mouth open.

"You have a fan." Maddie lifted her head and sniffed. "Why does the house smell so good?"

"Lasagna. My special recipe."

She put her hand over her chest. "I'm dead, aren't I? Dead and gone to heaven."

"Am I part of your heaven?"

"Only if you bring a case of chocolate with you."

"Mom," Zach said, "there's no food in heaven."

She looked down at his serious face. "How do you know?"

"The Bible doesn't say there is."

"But isn't everything good supposed to be in heaven?"

Zach's mouth worked as he pondered this new concept of heaven, his nose wrinkling. "Maybe. Can I have ice cream in heaven?"

"What flavor?"

He grinned. "All the flavors."

"Absolutely."

"Mr. Logan," Chloe piped up. "Are you a movie star?"

At Logan's expression of astonishment, Maddie turned a laugh into a snort.

"He's not a movie star," Zach said. "A movie star wouldn't live in our house."

"Is he going to be your new daddy?"

Maddie's desire to laugh whooshed right out of her chest. "No," she said firmly. "Mr. Logan is just...staying here temporarily."

"He's writing a book," Zach said. "Mom's helping him."

Chloe's eyes widened again. "A book about what?"

Maddie turned to him, and so did Zach. Logan stared at her, clearly telling her with his eyes that she should take this question.

"It's like *Puss in Boots*, only with people," she said.

"No cats?" Chloe's mouth turned down. "I like cats in books."

"There might be a cat in it," Logan said.

"I have a dog. Would you like to put a dog in it?" Chloe gave him a heart-melting smile.

"I'll see what I can do. Do you have a preference?"

"Huh?"

"He wants to know what kind of dog you want," Zach said.

"My dog's gray. Her name's Sweetie Pie. I love her, and she loves me. She's this high." She held out her hand to her knee.

"If I put a dog in it, I'll certainly consider naming it Sweetie Pie. How about we discuss this over dinner?"

"Okay. I have to go potty first."

He stepped back. "You go ahead and do that."

She scampered off.

"I don't have to pee," Zach said.

"Put your backpack away then wash your hands," Maddie said.

He scampered off.

"Just talking to them for five minutes tires me," Logan said. "I don't know how teachers do it."

"They should get hazard pay." She took a deep breath. "Thanks for making dinner."

"I had a spurt of energy. Don't expect it every day."

"I don't expect anything from you. If you'll excuse me, I'll change. I might even go potty, too."

His lips curved up, but his eyes were so dark they looked navy. "How long will Zach's friend be with us?"

"Her mom picks her up about seven. I don't know how good I'll be at thinking up a story tonight. I'm pretty tired."

"A story a night. That's our deal." He gazed at her with a slight smile, and she had the feeling he wanted her to get annoyed or even angry at him. Wanted her to glare and to say cutting words.

She didn't know why he was like this. If it was because of her or the kids. Or maybe it had nothing to do with her. It could be he always got this way when he made lasagna. Or maybe he'd heard from his dark queen. All she knew for sure was that she was not going to respond in kind.

"You'll get your story." She lowered her voice, not taking her gaze from his. "You're not the Big, Bad Wolf, though you might like to think you are. You shoveled the snow and made dinner."

"It was exercise. I like to move, I like to eat. I like doing other things , too."

"It was still kind of you."

"Kind?" The tension left his face, changing to a sensuality that froze her as he reached out to touch her hair, and his fingers brushed her cheek. A spark shot straight to her lower belly, and her breath caught, her semblance of serenity whizzing out of her. His eyes glowed, as if there were a flame in them. She'd never seen blue eyes before that looked so warm.

"Anything I do isn't out of kindness." His warm voice wrapped around her, like a velvet blanket. "When you get around to looking me up, everything you read about me that's bad, believe it."

She stepped back from him. She needed space to keep from melting into a puddle. "When I get around to it?" She managed to speak with her voice only a little breathless. "Are you kidding? I looked you up first thing this morning."

"So now you know the worst."

"I read a lot of innuendos, but you managed to stay out of the public eye." Except for his photos with actress Olivia Verdine. If he was sex personified in a male form, the dark-haired woman clinging to his arm in every picture was his female counterpoint, leaving men staring at her with their jaws open.

Taking a deep breath, she wiped the images out of her mind before continuing. "Your accomplishments are impressive. You produced six films, and two arc among my favorites."

He stilled. "Five were from other people's screenplays, not mine. And believe this: what people accomplish in films doesn't mean they're better than anyone else."

"You're constantly telling me how bad you are, but a really bad man would try to convince me he was good."

"Maybe I'm using reverse psychology."

"On me?" She frowned. "Why? It doesn't make sense."

His eyes roamed up and down her, but since she was wearing black slacks and a blue sweater that was five years old and machine washable—and she didn't want to think how old her bra was—she didn't even flinch.

Then his gaze continued up to her eyes and stayed there. "You don't know how...unusual you are."

"'Unusual' is a synonym for 'odd,' so if you're trying to flatter me, it's not working."

"'Unusual' could also be a synonym for 'rare.'"

She let her breath out in a puff. "You see, that's why I can't believe what you're saying. I'm not rare. There are millions of women like me." She held up her hand to stop him from interrupting. "I'm not putting myself down. I think I'm just fine as I am, but I know what I am, and that's someone who's down-to-earth and does what needs to be done. Don't make any more of me than that."

Before he could say anything more, she hurried away.

She didn't know where that...*stuff* he'd said about her came from.

She almost liked it better yesterday when she was afraid he'd call the sheriff on her.

On the other hand, if it weren't for Zach, she would have sex with him.

If he asked her... But every once in a while when she looked at him, his eyes darkened, and heat stole beneath her skin....

But Zach was here, and so that was that.

7

S he walked away, but it was a small house, and the devil seemed to have gotten into him.

Not the first time, and he doubted it would be the last.

When she returned in jeans and a blue sweatshirt, he flirted subtly as she set the table. She gave him that *look* again. As if he were a useless but harmless insect she couldn't swat away.

She amused him. But more than that, he liked her. And she kept him from thinking about *her*. His enchantress, his dark queen. The woman whom no other could match.

Olivia would laugh at him if she overheard his conversation with Maddie. She would tell him not to raise the serious young woman's hope.

Not that Maddie seemed to be affected by him, though he knew if he pushed hard enough, he could have her. He'd seen it more in the way that she'd sometimes avoided his gaze than the way she'd looked at him. And when he'd touched her face, she'd jerked away from him, and he knew she'd felt the same spark as him, their bodies calling to each other.

Biology, pure and simple—though there'd been nothing pure about his thoughts, just simple. The same thing most men would feel with an attractive woman. Hell, sometimes even a woman who wasn't attractive. Sometimes all a man cared about was the looks, but Logan needed something more.

Maddie had something more.

He was tempted...but her son complicated things. He didn't consider himself a good man—far from it. But there were some things he didn't do. In addition, she was living in his house, and if they had a short affair, getting her out could get awkward.

During dinner, he held himself back—no flirting in front of the kids. Instead, he observed the two kids and Maddie as if they were specimens from another planet. He'd been a child with busy parents. They'd loved him, but they both had had jobs and interests they'd enjoyed. He didn't recall feeling neglected. He'd just felt as though they didn't need him. Their lives were complete without him.

His mother remembered his childhood differently. She said he was independent, even as a small child.

Though there had been his dog.... When he'd lost Einy, it had been the first time his heart had broken. It had taken him years to get over the loss.

Even now, thinking about Einy, sorrow scraped out a hollow place in his chest.

He didn't love easily, but when he did, it lasted forever. He suspected if he had time to think a few minutes as he lay dying, he would close his eyes and picture Einy waiting for him in whatever place he was about to end up—whether it was up with the angels or down with the devil.

The doorbell interrupted his thoughts. Zach's friend jumped up, eager to go home with her mother, and Maddie strode to the door. Logan disappeared, heading up to his room. Better to not get cozy with the neighbors.

62

He remained in the bedroom with his phone off. Before coming to Angel Lake, he'd told his so-called friends he was going to be offline, and so far he hadn't checked his normal online sites. He sat at his computer now and looked at the second scene of the screenplay he'd started this morning. It was a black comedy about a man who found a woman in his house. Sleeping in his bed like Goldilocks.

Only in his book, the intruder wasn't a child, and the homeowner didn't have a wife or a baby.

The golden-haired girl in the original tale had to have known when she'd broken into the house that she was committing a trespass. He always did think the real Goldilocks got off lightly. That a real bear would have eaten her.

In his screenplay, the intruder would have to pay.

As he fleshed out what he'd written earlier today, voices drifted into his room, Maddie talking in Zach's bedroom, too far away to hear the words. The voices paused and, as he stopped breathing to hear better, he clearly heard the snitch of a door closing.

Zach had gone to bed.

His pulse quickened. His nostrils flared, as if sniffing the air for her scent.

Like a hunter, he thought. Or the anti-hero in his screenplay.

He'd told himself earlier that he wouldn't act on his libido—but that was in the daytime, and this was night. The sun disappeared at night and, apparently, so did his few scruples.

***

The other shoe fell.

That was the thought in Maddie's mind when he came downstairs as she was trying to find a show on TV in which men were *not* saying stupid things to each other in the mistaken belief that it was funny; in which woman were *not* being assaulted, chased, or horribly killed; in which housewives in full makeup and five-inch heels were *not* bullying each other.

She'd finally found her comfort station as he stepped into the living room, where he obviously was taking up too much air, because she felt a whoosh of oxygen leave her body. And she did not like it.

"HGTV?" he asked. "You planning on renovating a house?"

"Not this one, so don't worry." She spared him a glance then nodded at the TV. "That's my perfect man."

"A contractor?"

"A *hunky* contractor. He fixes things and has better taste than I do."

"He's probably gay."

If it were anyone else saying that, she would wonder if he was jealous. Though why not him?

The thought cheered her, even as she wished it wouldn't. If not for Zach, she would pack up and leave this place. She was only staying here because she didn't want to uproot him. "Are you ready for your story for the night?"

"When your heartthrob is on TV?"

She leaned her elbow on the arm of the chair then

rested her chin in her palm. She was so tired she might fall asleep in the middle of tonight's story. "I'll settle for seeing him in my dreams."

"We don't have the same dreams."

"I can imagine what yours are like."

He raised his right eyebrow and lowered his voice. "If you could, you would be running scared."

"Did anyone tell you you're a drama queen?"

He stilled. For a second, she wondered if she'd gone too far.

But what the hell. If she'd gone this far, why not go further?

"Why are you trying to scare me away?"

"Because you're a mother who cares for her son. And because that son is tucked in his bed, sleeping." He leaned in closer. "And because you want me as much as I want you."

She sat back. But not too far back. She didn't want him to think he frightened her. Didn't want him to think he was right. "I couldn't do anything with you, either. You'd always know you'd be second choice."

His eyes narrowed, and she could've sworn she felt a freezing blast of wind whistle through the room. "And who's first?"

"You forgot about the hunky contractor already?"

He blinked, as if he'd gone to a dark place and, in that instant, he stepped out of it. "If you'd like"—he lowered his voice so it curled around her—"I could show you my saw and hammer."

"That would impress me so much. Will you let me hold them as you undress?"

His lips didn't curve, but laugh lines crinkled around his eyes. "What do you plan on doing with the hammer and the saw?"

"You don't want to ruin the surprise, do you?"

He straightened. "You are something else. I'm getting a drink."

"A cold one, I hope. With lots of ice. Next time, don't try to seduce me."

"I didn't mean to. I told myself I wouldn't." He frowned then headed to the kitchen.

She stood and followed him to the kitchen, telling him to look in the cupboard above the stove hood where she kept her booze. Unlike her, he was able to reach it without climbing on a stool.

She resented that, even though she knew it didn't make sense. "So you were thinking about having sex with me but decided not to?"

He took out a bottle of brandy she'd never opened. She'd gotten it three years ago, a Christmas present from Caroline.

"Too many complications," he said.

"That's me. Complicated."

He looked sideways at her, his left eyebrow cocked. "You're not complicated. You're as clear as glass."

"I guess I am." She leaned against the wall, crossing her arms as she watched him open the top easily while she always struggled to open jars and bottles, her teeth gritted as she made grunting noises. Nice to know Mr. Supercilious had a useful skill besides shoveling snow and making a great lasagna. "My major purpose is to not lose my present job and not screw up my next job."

"Already thinking of the next job. You sound like a... Never mind."

"A working, single parent." She heard the toughness in her tone, the think-what-you-want-and-stuff-it attitude. "That's what I sound like. I got my masters in business this last summer. The town administrator is retiring this January, and I'm taking over."

"You're ambitious."

"Yes, and I'm proud of it. And..." She pushed away from the wall, and the bravado seeped out of her. "I wouldn't have done it without you."

"Do you have a glass? Or should I say, do *I* have a glass?"

"How do you want it?" She stepped to a cupboard and opened it.

"Neat."

She grabbed a glass that she used for Zach's orange juice then handed it to Logan. "I've been wanting to say something to you."

His eyes turned wary, but he nodded, as if giving her permission to speak. But she didn't need his permission. This was something she should have said yesterday.

"Living here is the reason I got the job. The townspeople trusted me because they thought you did. Well, not you specifically, but whoever inherited your grandmother's house. Because of that trust, Zach goes to a great school, and we have a great future." She hesitated, because that wasn't all she had to say to him. "But I took advantage of this much longer than I should have. I should have left sooner, and I didn't."

He held the brandy bottle with one hand, the glass

with another. Not saying anything. Forcing her to go on.

"I'm grateful, and I'm sorry."

"If you'd left," he said, "who would've helped Sarah and all the other people make it through their hard times?"

She looked away. "It's true, but I was doing it without your permission. It's your home, and using it that way is a form of stealing."

"You look tired." His voice was rough. "Go to bed."

She realized that as she'd talked, she'd stepped back against the cupboard, pressing against it. She pushed away from the cupboard, her head up. "I'm not that tired. We made a deal, and I'm sticking to it. You want me to tell you a story, then let's do it."

He poured brandy into his glass. "I think I'll need this. You want some?"

She hesitated then shook her head. Around him, she seemed to lose her shut-mouth, turn-on-brain button. Anything alcoholic might make her talk more and think even less. "I'll do better justice to the story without alcohol."

"But what if it's not justice I want?"

Good thing she didn't have any alcohol, because she might tell him she wanted the same thing. "Then that's your problem," she said.

He laughed, but there was an edge to it, and tension sliced through her body. A combination of restlessness and need that made her get up and leave the room like he was Satan and she was an angel in trouble. Only they both knew she was no angel.

***

"My story is a derivative of Sleeping Beauty." She sipped the hibiscus tea she'd made because hibiscus was supposed to be good for her heart—and her heart was beating way too fast. Once again, he sat on the recliner, and she sat on the couch. This time, Ginger draped her purring body over Maddie's jean-covered legs.

"I'm going to guess the beauty is a former, pregnant college student," Logan said.

"Really? That's your guess? You try going into a coma with a baby in your belly."

"I'll pass on the baby in the belly. Go on."

"My story starts with a young girl running through the woods. Her name is....Jazlyn."

"By herself?"

"Not quite. Rabbits and squirrels bounded and scampered alongside her. Bluebirds and cardinals flew above her."

"No butterflies?"

"Many. Hundreds of butterflies. In all the colors of the rainbow."

"Were Jazlyn and her menagerie, winged and otherwise, going to grandmother's house?"

"No, the young girl was training for a half marathon." She narrowed her eyes at him. "Are you going to let me tell you the story my way?"

He sat back, holding out his hands in apology.

She inhaled to relax herself and sat back. "She stumbled over something. Luckily she landed on the ground covered with leaves—though her palms did sting.

But she got to her feet, wiped her hands on her skintight runner's pants, then looked behind her to see what she'd tripped over. It was a man. She recognized him from the tabloid papers she'd seen at grocery stores. Though his hair was dark brown, almost black"—she leaned forward to stare at his face until Ginger squawked a protest—"instead of golden, he was the fairest prince in the land. His eyes were the color of the plume of a bluebird. His lips begged women to kiss him. And his form..." She sighed and allowed her gaze to dwell on his lips curving upward, then she raked her gaze very slowly down his body then very slowly up again. "It was just right. The kind of figure young girls dreamed of on their Prince Charming."

Ginger squawked again, this time a demand for Maddie to pet her. Used to her cat's demands, Maddie glanced down at her orange and white cat and decided she was surrounded by beauty tonight.

Then she gazed back at Logan's smirking face and thought, *at least in appearance.*

Yet he hadn't called the sheriff and hadn't thrown her, Zach, and Ginger out of the house and into the snow. That counted for something.

"One woman especially became enamored of him," she continued. "Sonya was his female counterpoint, so beautiful that when she was very young, she'd been called by a magazine the 'Fairest Woman in the Land.'"

He stilled. Though he didn't change position, she saw his body tighten, and he held his body motionless, as if breathing shallowly.

In the same tone she used to tell bedtime stories to

70

Zach, she said, "She took it as her due, because her mirror told her they were right. But this magazine named a new 'Fairest Woman in the Land' every year. It wasn't fair, because this second year, she was even more beautiful and glowing. More exquisite. But despite her obvious superiority, the magazine voted another woman most fair. The year after that, it was another woman. And then another year and another Fairest in the Land. Because she'd been recognized so young, years were passing, and she feared people thought she was old.

"It infuriated Sonya, so that her dark eyes snapped and her mind seethed." She paused, taking a breath before continuing. "Like a witch's brew in a pot over a fire. She had to do something."

She gazed at Logan. His face was so smooth it could've been a mask, his full lower lip flattened to a line.

"The day after the latest issue of the magazine came out, she opened the magazine and saw that she was number sixteen most fair. Sixteen! Bloody sixteen! The editors were blind, they were prejudiced. Perhaps they'd been bought off, though her manager swore to her that if she tried to bribe the magazine and got caught, the world would snicker at her.

"She had to do something. That night, she went to a party, and she saw the prince. He was a star in the room. The next new thing. As she'd once been. And the most wonderful thing was that he didn't know he was a star." She took another deep breath. "She immediately saw this handsome, young prince was her equal in beauty. And you know what she did then?"

"I think so," he said, and his voice was harsh.

71

She replied in a whisper, bending forward, as if they were telling secrets. "She enthralled him."

When a visible shudder went through him, she felt slightly sick. Not throwing up but wanting to.

She forced herself to continue. "In fact, that's what he told people, his smile twisted as if pulling a joke on them. Only this prince knew that the joke was on him, and it was poison in his soul."

"I thought this was about a sleeping beauty." His voice sounded like it had been dragged through the bottom level of hell. "It sounds like your guy is awake."

"Maybe his mind and his mouth were awake—and even his body—but his heart was asleep. It still pumped blood, but the place where love and hope and wonder should have been was closed and locked up, with a large *Keep Out* sign tacked on. The only one admitted was Sonya, his enchantress."

"Is this the pre-Grimm version?"

Hot tears came to her eyes. She blinked them back, sorry she'd started this story, but she kept going, compelled to finish. "No, this is the real-life version."

"What about the happy ending?"

"Have you forgotten that you prefer the unhappy ending? Besides, this isn't a real fairy tale. It's more like real life. And things changed during real life. Even though Sonya had stolen his heart and locked it away, the prince didn't always obey her. And without his heart, he was known for producing films without emotion. Films with violence. Films with intelligence. Films that opened the darkest and rawest emotions. But the heart of his films was missing."

His jaw clenched, and his eyes glittered icily.

She didn't know where all this came from—except gossip Internet sites and IMBD—and she thought that maybe she should keep her mouth shut. But that train had already chugged out of the building, so now all she could do was continue and hope it didn't crash and burn.

The only problem was she didn't know where this train ride would end.

"Though Sonya retained her beauty, the meaty roles she craved were going to women with less beauty and less years. Every birthday was like a stab in her heart, which, to be honest, had never been that big. She took precautions that her looks didn't change, so she was as beautiful as ever. But the freshness was gone. She still glowed, but it was artificial. Too bright and too harsh. And no matter how much she tried to disguise it, the darkness in her soul showed like smog in the air. So she did what enchantresses did everywhere."

She looked expectantly at Logan, who stared stonily back, not blinking. She sighed. "You must be a hell of a poker player."

Still, he stared. Still, he said nothing.

"This was a bad idea," she said. "Very, very bad."

8

He wouldn't let her see that anything she said bothered him. "You're getting away from the story. Why was the prince in the woods? Sleeping?"

"Not asleep. In a coma. He'd wandered into the woods on his way home to his grandmother's house, and being so far from the keeper of his heart, he'd fallen into a coma. But when Jazlyn fell on top of him, it woke the prince—"

"The jolt did it?" he asked.

"Her legs fell across his naughty parts. That part of his anatomy had never been frozen."

"So now the prince is minus a heart but plus an erection."

"Yes." Her voice flattened. "He told Jazlyn if she had sex with him, he would buy her a house."

"This story is starting to sound familiar."

She avoided his eyes as she continued. "Jaz immediately saw his heart was frozen. She'd recently been with a weasel disguised as a man, and the weasel had stolen from her. So she wasn't falling for another pretty face—"

"Not to mention his naughty parts."

"Forget his naughty parts."

"So far, that's my favorite part of this story."

"I'm not surprised. Anyway, she refused him. She told him she would only have sex with a man whose heart wasn't frozen. And then she ran away from him."

Stopping, she looked down at Ginger, still on her lap, and drew her hand down the cat's spine.

"He chased her?" he asked, wanting now to know the end of the story.

She looked up at him. "You weren't listening. I told you in the beginning that she was a marathon runner. He was a dilettante who hung around at parties with his dark goddess, acting cool. How could he catch up to her?"

Ginger meowed, as if in agreement, and jumped off her lap.

"He turned back," she said, "and went to search for his enchantress to reclaim his heart."

"What about her? Jazlyn?"

"The next day, she ran the marathon, and she came in tenth. Number eleven was a hunky contractor, and they started to date."

"She's not Princess Charming then?"

"She's a commoner, and commoners don't end up with princes."

"Not even when the prince wants the commoner?"

"Princes always want what they shouldn't have. In any case, the story's about him, not her. She woke him from his coma, but he has to find his heart himself. But I can't tell you the rest tonight. It's a long story."

"Shorten it. You promised a story a night."

She yawned, and her eyes watered.

He stood. "Forget what I just said. Finish it tomorrow."

She stood, and her expression reminded him of a bulldog's. "I'll keep to my agreement and finish it now.

I'll just say he had many adventures, including ones with a midget, a hooker, a singer, a pie maker, a yoga instructor, and finally, he met Sonya, his enchantress, again. And he looked at her, and it was like looking at an acquaintance. And only then did he realize the truth."

As she stopped, he had a hard time keeping his eyes on her face, because her breasts were heaving, and she was still upset. And so many women he'd known in California had breasts that no longer heaved. So he thought, what the hell, why not look? And he raked his eyes down to her breasts and thought about holding them in his hands, how soft they would be and how their weight would feel in his palms and fingers, and how he would put his mouth to one and then the other.

"What is the truth?" he finally asked, raising his eyes to hers that sparked with anger.

"The truth," she snapped out the words, "is that he had the power to unfreeze his heart all along."

"Isn't that what the good witch said to Dorothy in Oz?"

"Yes." She smiled. "And the good witch was right. Now if you'll excuse me, the story is over, and I'm going to bed."

He watched her march out of the living room, and he thought there might be some truth in the story, but it wasn't the bit about his heart that was the truth, it was the bit about his naughty parts.

Or, as he preferred, his fun parts.

They had awakened big-time.

***

As Maddie entered her bedroom, she was shaking, and her skin was hot. She looked at herself in the dresser mirror. Her cheeks were flushed, and her pupils were dilated like an addict who'd just had a hit. But her hit was the man who owned this house, breathing the same air with him, being so close to him that she could smell the scent of musk and man. And if she concentrated hard, she could even feel the heat.

She'd started the story to make him uncomfortable. A petty revenge for making her tell him a story tonight.

It had backfired on her, karma biting her in the ass. She'd ended up making herself uncomfortable, while he'd been as cool as a Popsicle.

She sat on the edge of her bed and put her heated face in her hands. Oh God, not a Popsicle. That was not an image she wanted stuck inside her mind.

Obviously it was time to date again. She was fairly young, her body had needs, and Logan was...Logan. He made her think of jaded heroes from romance novels, radiating cynicism and pheromones. Any straight woman her age would be excited by him.

On her break tomorrow, she needed to make a list of all the unattached men in the right age range who she knew. Or perhaps she should talk to friends and let them know she was on the hunt. Or maybe the best idea was to join an online dating site.

This time she would choose her lover carefully, with her mind and not her body. She would make lists of what she wanted in a man. This time she would do it the smart way.

***

His human's scent had disappeared. Dog wanted to howl, but too many other dogs would hear him. Though it was dark, he kept running in the same direction, hoping to catch the smell again.

Freezing air and snow pellets gusted at him, and still he ran. Faster and faster, to keep the blood rushing inside him, warming him.

Another smell came to him. He recognized it, all his hunting instincts on alert.

Earlier today, he'd eaten a mouse. It had not tasted good, but it was food and filled his belly. The snow was his water.

He knew should find a place to sleep where it was warm and safe, but a stronger need overwhelmed him, pushing him to run faster.

This need had been an open ache inside his heart since he could remember. First there had been his mother and his brothers and sisters. He'd been happy with them. Yet there had been the ache in his heart that cried out for something more. For *him,* Dog knew now. The human whose smell was gone. No other man or woman would be the right one.

Another gust whipped at him, colder than before, and he realized the pads of his paws were freezing.

He couldn't wait. He needed to find shelter. Now.

He took another step, and that's when his front paw came down on a rock covered with snow. The stone rolled away, and he fell down hard.

Something in his leg pulled and twisted.

He howled, a cry of pain.

He stopped his howl—too late. Any predator within earshot would already be racing toward him, looking for easy prey.

Pushing up with his other three legs, he struggled onto his feet. He stood in one place for a moment, wobbling, before taking a step forward.

He fell again. Pain burned through him, and he whimpered, unable to stop himself.

Then he pushed up to his feet again and stepped forward.

When he fell again, this time he held back the whimper.

He took a step and another step. The ground was uneven, and he lurched forward. A smell of cows drifted to him, and he angled toward it. Where there were cows, there was a barn. Shelter. Heat.

Dog reached the barn finally, though it seemed to take a long, long time. There was a light on inside the building. He smelled the scent of human. Before he could investigate, a door opened. Light spilled out over him, and a man turned to look at him. Scents of cows and cats and wheat came out of the barn as the man stared at him, and he stared back.

Then it began to snow harder and faster.

He took a step forward.

The man didn't say anything. Didn't move.

He took another step forward. And another. With each step, his body staggered.

Then he was inside, on the barn floor, and he heard the man on a phone, saying "hurt" and "dog" as he tumbled to the floor, and pain streaked through his leg.

He was aware of eyes on him, the cows placid, the cats streaking away then stopping, realizing he wasn't any threat.

But most of all, he was aware of the heat that blanketed him, coming off of the cows, and he was aware of the human looking down at him.

And he was tired. So tired. His eyes closed despite the danger, despite the strangeness, despite the pain. So he laid his head down and, not knowing what was going to happen, he slept.

9

MUST HAVES:

Enjoy children
Be single
Be under age 35 30 35
Work—have a job or own a business
Kindness
Gentleness
Sense of humor
Cleanliness
Honesty
Loyalty
A one-woman man
Be there when I need him
Love cats

WOULD LIKE TO HAVE:

Good-looking (or not really ugly—though ugly cute is okay)
Tall (but shorter isn't a deal breaker)
Great body (or just take care of himself physically)
Healthy
Lots of money (hahaha)
Be generous with his money (hahahahahaha)
Give great massages
Give foot rubs

Be an equal partner in raising children (move to 'must have' list?)
Will take care of me when (if) I'm sick
Likes to dance

As Maddie hurried into the living room with a mug of hot chocolate and one of tea, she saw Logan leaning over her netbook on the small Queen Anne desk in the corner, reading her lists. She jerked to a stop then rushed forward.

Hot liquid swished over her hands. Swearing silently, she set the mugs on a newspaper on the coffee table to soak up any spilled liquid. She straightened, her spine stiff, her chin up. He'd already turned to face her, his movements unhurried, one side of his mouth twisted up.

"That's private." Her voice shook, and she swore silently again. With him around, she should loop the swear words through her mind every twenty minutes.

His left eyebrow cocked. "You mean the lists aren't about me?"

"If you really thought they were, you'd be out of here in the next five minutes."

"Have you forgotten whose house it is?"

She crossed her arms. "I guess I did. Should I start packing?"

"You're insecure."

"I think I have reason to be insecure."

"Guilty conscience?"

She felt herself flush.

"If you had to do it all over again, would you do it differently?" he asked, and his voice was different.

Kinder but in an impersonal way that made her feel stupidly sad.

"Probably not. I helped a lot of people."

"How many did you shelter here? More than three?"

"Never mind." She held her head high. "No one harmed anything. And if you threaten to kick me out over that or anything else again, I'll make arrangements to leave immediately."

He stared at her, his eyelids half down, his expression unreadable. "I won't do it again. In any case, I'm not kicking a mom and her kid out of the house before Christmas. As for your lists, if you want them to remain private, don't leave them where I can read them."

She walked around him to get to the desk. Though she didn't like it, he was right. As she shut off her netbook, he didn't move to make room for her, standing only a couple inches away. She forced her hand not to twitch.

"Did you leave your lists there on purpose?" he asked.

Her hands shook after all as she closed the lid. She snapped around. "No. Now, do you want your story tonight or don't you?"

"Not when you're in that mood."

"My moods have nothing to do with it."

"Your words are coming out like bullets. Hot and deadly."

"If they were, you'd be lying on the floor, bleeding over the carpet." She gestured at the tan carpet. "Yet you're still standing."

His eyes gleamed. "If you lay on the carpet next to me, I wouldn't mind."

Since he still wasn't moving, she stepped back. "You're in love with another woman."

"What's that got to do with sex?"

"Are all men like you?"

"Pretty much."

"No wonder the world is in such bad shape."

"No arguments here."

"We agreed not to have any complications."

"I know, and you'd be a huge one."

His words stopped her. Why would she be a huge one? In a way, that was a compliment—

His smile became less sexual, more mocking. "Because of Zach."

"Of course." She smiled stiffly. It felt as if he could see into her mind or, worse, her emotions, and see her attraction for him—her very reluctant attraction—which he was using for his amusement. "Are you ready to listen to tonight's story?"

He didn't reply right away, staring at her, and she stood stiffly, taking it. This was her payback for living here for too many years.

But, damn it, she would only stand still for so long.

In that second, she made her decision. Christmas was coming in five weeks. She'd look for a place to move to in January.

"If you want to skip tonight's story…" She reached for her netbook, ready to take it to her room along with her tea.

"Stay." He stepped back. "Tell me your story."

***

"This is a true story," she said.

A smile grew inside him, and he reminded himself not to goad her too far. She amused him, and he didn't want her to walk out before he was bored by her stories. "True stories usually don't have a good ending."

"That should fit your criteria of unhappy endings. Besides, there's always an unhappy ending in fairy tales. In the original Cinderella—the pre-Grimm one—I believe the two stepsisters had to cut off their heels to fit into Cindy's slippers. Just think of them, hobbling around for the rest of their lives."

"I'm from L.A. If small feet were the rage, I can name you a few thousand women who'd happily pay money to have someone slice off their heels."

She made a face. "My story does *not* have anyone cutting off a heel. I'm changing a few details, but it started in Chicago. There were two little girls. One watched a lot of princess movies when she was young. The other preferred to watch movies—and read books— in which the girl killed the dragon and fought off the bad people. One entered beauty pageants, the other took karate lessons and started winning in tournaments."

"Do they have names?"

"One was Lily, and one was Rose."

"Rose must be the intrepid girl," he said, "because roses have thorns."

She didn't acknowledge his insightfulness. The name would fit Maddie, too, he thought. He settled back into the recliner. So did Maddie, who, tonight, was a mad woman.

The thought made him smile.

Her voice settled into a storytelling rhythm, her tone smooth and compelling as she told him about the two girls growing up and Lily marrying her prince. Though he didn't have an actual title, his father was the CEO and chairman of his own commodity brokerage firm, and her husband was being groomed to take over.

While Lily decorated her lakefront mansion, Rose was traveling the world, treating men like they were takeout meals. When it was convenient and she felt the hunger, she used them. And when she was done with them...then she was done.

"What was her profession?" he asked.

"A photographer and blogger. She wasn't famous, but she burned brightly and had a devoted following who bought her picture books. And every picture had a story."

He nodded. She was giving him images in his mind in which Rose looked slightly like Maddie, though her hair was redder and longer and wilder, and she was taller and leaner, her body hard with muscles. Not his type, but he wouldn't mind being her takeout meal.

"They were both happy, or so Rose thought. Until she noticed that her sister's voice sounded funny. Too chirpy. Like a bad actress. She tried to find out more, but Lily insisted everything was fine. That her prince was wonderful, and she was learning his world to fit in and be a credit to him and his company."

She stopped to take a deep breath, and he realized that the atmosphere in the living room had changed. Three lamps were still lit, but in the last couple minutes, the room seemed darker and murkier, and her expression was stern. The face of a judge.

"Rose immediately kicked her latest meal out of her hotel room. She cancelled her appointments, bought plane tickets, and flew back to Chicago, which was halfway around the world." She paused and raised her eyes to him. The air between them seemed to liquefy.

"A long trip," he said, not releasing her gaze. Her face had tensed and hardened. He imagined Rose's face had the same look.

"She had a lot of planning to do."

"What kind of planning?"

"You can't rush the story." She smiled at him, and it was a cunning smile. An urge stirred inside him to describe that smile, and the block that had been inside him for too many years crumbled as if it were made out of old cheese.

Now he had a block of new cheese.

"Go on. Tell me more."

She narrowed her eyes at him. "You're staring at me like you're trying to see through my clothes."

No clothes in my mind, he thought. Though right now it wasn't her body that was naked, it was her soul.

And they both gave him an erection. He wasn't going to tell her, though he suspected she wouldn't be surprised.

"It's the nature of the devil," he said.

"I'm not blaming the devil. I'm blaming the man."

"I'm getting turned on by your story. Don't stop now." He needed to hear this story. Needed to watch her face as she spoke, to see her expression change, to see her sit in one place and make his numbed heart hammer and his muscles tense.

It wasn't only his writer's block that had crumbled.

She spoke, telling him about the sisters' reunion. How Rose's brother-in-law invited her to stay with them, his arm around Lily's shoulders and his eyes glittering with possession. Rose smiled and acted as if she didn't notice her sister seemed like a caricature of a 1950s TV housewife. All she needed was an apron, though an apron wouldn't go well with the stripper heels Lily wore even in her oversized mansion.

"That night, Rose slept well," Maddie said. "She knew she needed sleep for what was going to come. The next morning, the prince said he was thinking of staying home to escort her around—as if she hadn't lived in the city for most of her life before her travels. But Rose put on her best smile, the one she used to disarm tribal chiefs and government officials. She told him how wonderful that would be. And then she bent forward and laid her hand on his arm, gazing up into his eyes, and told him how lucky Lily was to have found a man like him."

Inhaling deeply, she stopped, her hazel eyes burning brighter than before. But it was an icy burning.

"He swallowed that?" Logan leaned toward her. "He didn't guess that she was playing him?"

"He believed her. After all, it's what his father taught him, and probably what his father's father taught him. That women were put on earth to serve men. Especially men with money and looks and a certain amount of charisma." Her gaze raked up and down him, and her lips pulled back from her teeth in a sneer.

A laugh built inside him, but he didn't say anything. He wanted badly to hear the end of the story—though he already guessed what it might be.

"So the prince went off to his father's brokerage—"

"Where he counted out his money."

A smile flicked on her face. "Yes. He loved counting out his money. Loved it almost as much as he loved torturing his wife. While he was gone, Rose got Lily to admit that the prince hurt her in ways that didn't leave any mark. That he had control of her money, and she'd signed a prenup that left her with nothing if she divorced him. He had to divorce her for her to get any money.

"Rose tried to get Lily to leave with her, saying she had enough money for both of them. But Lily was as stubborn as she was beautiful and as Rose was brave. Finally, Rose nodded and said she would visit old friends. She was gone for hours, and she returned before dinner. They waited for the prince who had planned to take them to a fundraising dinner. But the prince didn't come and didn't come. And Lily wouldn't call him, because it—"

A yawn stopped her, a giant-sized one.

"Because it made him angry," he said. "Go to bed. Finish it tomorrow."

She sat up straight. "Our deal was a story a night. I'll finish now. I'll skip a few parts and just say that a call came from a hospital, and the prince was there. He'd been attacked and had bones broken in several places. They rushed to the hospital, and the prince's father, the king, was there. The king said the police left already, that a slight masked man had attacked the prince with martial arts moves. The masked man had claimed that the king's investment firm had cheated a sister with their stock transfers. Before the masked man left, he announced in front of witnesses that the prince and the king would soon be met by a demand from his sister. If they didn't give him money, he'd return. Next time, the prince would never walk again.

"As the father said that, he was shaking. The father loved two things in life: money and his son. He'd raised his son to be just like him. Rose told him that she was once a part of Chicago's martial arts community, and she could understand why he was so fearful for his son. That, theoretically, she knew a few ways to kill a man in less than one second of time."

Maddie paused again to sip her tea. As she sipped then set the mug down, Logan remained still, not even picking up his own mug of hot chocolate. Silently urging her to finish.

"The king was not a stupid man," she said. "He asked what Lily wanted. Rose said a divorce, even as Lily tried to say she wanted nothing, her voice a whine as her sedated husband lay on the hospital bed. The king ignored her, and so did Rose as they hammered out a deal. The next day, there was enough money transferred to Lily's bank account for her to live the rest of her life. She saw a lawyer in the morning, and in the afternoon, she and Rose packed up and took a plane to a town in Sicily where they moved in with a lover of Rose's who would never let any man touch a hair on her sister's head without Rose's permission."

She stopped again and frowned at her tea. "Next time, I'm going to drink wine."

"Is the story over?" he asked.

"Not yet." She raised her eyes to his. "Though the traditional news quickly backed off from the king and the prince, the alternative news weeklies asked searching questions about the company's financial dealings. And what was worse was that the tabloids wouldn't leave the prince alone."

"They heard about the way he'd treated his wife?"

"No. They wanted to know why his assailant had chopped off the heels of his feet."

It was good that he wasn't holding his hot chocolate because he would've spit it out as he threw his head back to laugh until his stomach hurt.

If nothing else, this woman entertained him.

Though there was something else. Maybe too much to dwell on. "You said there would be no chopping off heels in this story."

"I couldn't have you guessing the ending, could I?" She got up, taking her tea with her, and headed to the kitchen.

"Are you getting wine?" he asked. "Get me a glass, too."

Not slowing, she said, "Get your own damn wine."

He laughed again, and inside him, exultation rose. Nothing had changed...but there was a shift inside him, and it felt like everything had changed.

And then the phone rang, the one ring that he allowed, playing the first notes of a song that was as familiar to him as oxygen.

And as poisonous as fire...

10

His ringtone sounded familiar, sexy yet shuddery. Maddie turned to see his expression close up.

Her. It had to be her. His dark enchantress. Or witch. Or whatever the hell he called her.

His jaw clenched, and hate fired through her. She stood for a moment, and his eyes met hers, and she saw hate in them, too.

Not for her, she thought, and maybe not for the caller. For himself. An addict's self-hate.

She could be imagining all this, but the sick sense in her throat was too real, and she snapped around and hurried into the kitchen, unable to look at him.

The phone rang twice again as she poured the tea into the sink then went to the refrigerator to pour herself a glass of wine. Adrenaline raced through her blood, as if she'd eaten too much sugar. And now that she stopped thinking about the ringtone, the name of the song popped into her mind. *Witchy Woman.*

Wondering if he'd answered on the last ring or if he was going to call his enchantress back, she took a swig of her wine, the refrigerator door still open. Like a guy, she thought. They stood in front of open refrigerators all the time. Why shouldn't women?

But the cold made her shiver, and a small noise brought her gaze to the side. Logan. He was leaning against the wall, watching her as if she were a robin in snow. With his eyes half hooded and his arms crossed, he looked more than ever like a leading man in a movie. Maybe a James Bond type, ready to kill a spy.

Or make love to the spy.

Her heartbeat speeded. Telling herself not to be a dork, she said, "I'll get you a glass of wine."

"Not wine." He headed to the cupboard where she kept the bottle of brandy he'd opened a previous evening. She went to a different cupboard and held a glass out to him. He took it, poured a few ounces of brandy into it, tipped his head back, and slugged the brandy down. Not saying a word, he poured another couple ounces.

Her gut twisted. She could see his torment. She reached out to comfort him—then pulled her arm back. Quietly, she set her almost half full wine glass on the counter then headed to her room.

Tomorrow she would call Kevin Spindlebottom, the local real estate agent and town board member. As far as she knew, there were no homes for sale in town except for a couple on the lake that she couldn't afford. This wasn't the time of year that people left their houses. They were settled in for the holidays.

She'd tell Kevin that as soon as he heard about a house for sale in her price range, he should get in touch with her. Right now she was open to just about anything. She just wanted to get out of here and away from Logan. Breathing the same air as him was bad for her heart.

***

A young girl entered the barn, and Dog lifted his head. "I want to see the dog!" the girl said.

The man told her to be careful, but she was already bending over Dog.

"What's your name? Huh? What's your name?" She rubbed the skin below his ear. Her breath smelled as fresh as her face looked.

A hunger awoke in the dog's stomach. Not for food. He always had that hunger, as if there were a big, empty hole in his belly. For almost as long as he could remember, he'd had that. But this was different—a hunger in his chest.

He leaned into her rubbing fingertips, his first eyelids pulling down.

"Don't pet him," a woman said, her voice sharp as she closed a door behind her, shutting out an icy wind. "He might have bugs."

Dog lifted his head. He smelled human food.

"Mom, it's too cold for ticks." The girl looked toward the woman who'd come into the barn.

"You don't know how long he's been running wild. He smells, and he's filthy." The woman handed the man the food and something else. "You shouldn't have let Kim come in. The dog might bite her."

"The dog won't bite her."

"Oh, you can read dogs' minds now?"

If it weren't for the food, the woman's voice would've made Dog slink to a corner of the barn to stay out of her way. But his stomach wanted that food. Wanted it badly.

It had been a long time since a human had given him food. A very long time.

"If it bites her," the man said, "I'll buy you that new fancy phone you want."

"Am I going to bet my daughter's life on a phone?" She slugged his arm.

A growl started in Dog's throat, and everyone looked at him.

The girl jumped up. "Mom, he doesn't like you hitting Daddy."

"I like this dog."

Dog could tell by the smile in the man's voice that this was good. He liked the man, too. The man was coming toward him with food in a pail. He knelt and put it in front of dog. Dog's leg hurt still, but he struggled to his feet.

"Something's wrong with his leg." The woman's voice softened then hardened again. "We can't keep a dog that's going to cost us a fortune in vet bills."

"I'll do what I can to fix him."

"What do you know about doctoring? You'll just mess up his leg."

Dog finished gobbling up the food and licked the bowl while the man said something to the woman, and the woman said something back, their words sounding like hard stones being thrown. When Dog looked up at the girl, she knelt next to him and hugged him tight.

Tears dripped onto the top of his head, and a long sigh whiffed through him and out his mouth. He wouldn't be able to leave. At least, not now.

The girl needed him, and his chest hurt again. He wouldn't be able to follow the smell and find his human. He had to stay with the girl.

11

Olivia was his drug, but Maddie with her nighttime stories was his antidote.

Every night for five days, the ringtones of "Witchy Woman" rang out, and every night, he held back from answering. Every note was like a string pulling him. As if Olivia were whispering to him, *"Come, pick it up, hear my voice, come under my spell again. You know you want to."*

If Olivia had called him during the daytime when Maddie was working, then he might weaken and answer. Anything to take a break from his struggles to write.

And without Maddie nearby, he might succumb to the pull, just to hear Olivia's sultry voice that promised nights of pleasure.

On the fourth night, Maddie asked him why he wasn't putting the phone on buzz. He looked at her for a long couple moments, and the color rose in her cheeks. But she didn't break her gaze, her mouth mulish, more stubborn than her cat.

He got up finally, the phone silent now, and went to his phone in the kitchen to turn off the ring. He'd left it there on purpose since the first night Olivia had called. Farther away from the temptation that gnawed at his chest.

With the phone off, he felt a sense of victory. A week ago, he couldn't have done that. It wasn't the distance that gave him the incentive. It was Maddie and her stare that dared him to turn off the damn phone.

When he returned, he nodded at Maddie to go on then sipped his brandy. Oddly enjoying the dirty look she gave him before she started her story, a defense against her attraction to him. He was an expert at this game that men and woman played, and she was only an amateur.

She started her tale about trees that could pull up their roots and walk, with gnomes and fairies. It sounded a lot like L.A. to him. All it was missing was a witch.

"And then the witch appeared," she said.

Laughter poured out of him while she glared her disapproval. His stomach hurt, and he slapped his thigh.

No one who knew him in L.A. would recognize him. He was known for his sophistication, not his guffaws.

That's when it hit him.

The ice that had kept his heart frozen for more than nine years was melting.

His laughter stopped abruptly, and he found himself staring at her while she looked back at him with her forehead creased in puzzlement.

He shared her confusion. What was happening to him? His chest felt too tight. He was having a hard time breathing, his lungs constricted.

"You don't like the story?" she asked.

He sucked air into his lungs but didn't answer for another breath. "I found the story amusing," he said.

"It's not supposed to be amusing." She snapped out the words like they were tacks in her mouth.

He slouched back in the recliner, feeling more himself. *This* was the man his old friends would recognize.

"I'll tell a different one," she said.

"I want to hear that one."

"You're being difficult."

"This isn't the first time I've been called that."

"I bet it isn't." She took a slug of beer. "Nor is it the first time you ignored it."

"I've gotta be me." He grinned.

She groaned. "Okay, I'll just quickly tell you what happened. The witch put a spell on the gnome."

"Why?"

"Because she didn't like gnomes in her garden."

"I can understand that. I bet he peeped through her window when she undressed."

"What kind of mind do you have? This is a *fairy tale*."

"Gnomes are males, right? Then he's peeping." He shrugged. "What else does he have to do in the garden? Watch zucchini grow?"

"He can watch the rabbits hump."

"Oh, what fun."

"You brought it up. Actually, he and the fairy might have something going on."

"The fairy isn't going out with a gnome."

"Why not?" she asked.

"Because she's beautiful with her gossamer wings and her tiny but perfect body. And the gnome has a white beard, dresses funny, and is short and stumpy."

"She lives in a forest, and she happens to like short, stumpy men. Okay?"

Her irritation brought back his amusement, and he cocked an eyebrow. "So she's a pervert. She could've had the tree man. When he's in his man-shape, he's tall and strong."

She smirked. "She's allergic to pollen."

He grinned, and she picked up the thread of the story, telling him about a fight between the fairy and the witch. He interrupted only once to tell her that he always liked a story with a cat fight.

She looked at him blandly. "I'll remember that next time. What you didn't know about the gnome is that the witch loved him, too. Contrary to your opinion, short and stumpy men are *greatly* admired in the fairy world."

"I suppose you're eager to tell me why."

"Not eager, but since you asked, they're known to be better in bed than someone who's..." She shrugged and gestured to him. "You know."

He sat straight up. "No, I don't know."

She raised her eyebrows. "Think about it. Gnomes are very good at pleasuring women. While men like the tree man"—she paused and stared pointedly at him—"are used to having women pleasure them."

"Thank you for enlightening me."

"Anytime. As the fairy and the witch fought, the gnome stepped between them and begged the fairy to leave the witch alone. That's when she realized that the gnome was enchanted by the witch."

His grin flattened to a line, growing still.

She stared at him. Daring him to stop her. "For years, the gnome has seen the witch as the most beautiful woman in the world. But then the witch goes away for a few weeks to help her sister because a house dropped on her head, and when she comes back, the gnome is hanging around with this skinny fairy with a magic wand. And the witch really hates magic wands. She thinks they're cheats."

"The witch has something there."

"The witch has her cauldron and her broom. An *electric* broom."

"An electric broom. That makes all the difference. That's real cheating."

"This is the world of magic. Electric brooms aren't welcome in fairyland. So let me tell you what happened, please."

"Is that a polite way of telling me to shut up?"

"Yes. Now, there was an epic battle between the witch and the fairy. I find battles boring, so I'll get to the dark moment, when the witch is zapping the fairy with her electric broom."

"Cheater."

"I'm glad you realized that and don't condone it."

"I'm all for cheating."

She rolled her eyes. "But then the power went out, and the fairy raised her wand—"

"Shouldn't the use of a wand be classified as cheating?"

"That's not cheating, that's magic." She stood. "May I finish?"

He gestured for her to go for it. She was glaring at him and holding up her beer. He didn't want it spilled on his lap.

She set down her beer on the table next to the sofa before continuing. "The fairy turned to the gnome and took the spell off of him. Faster than the witch could blink, the gnome stepped in front of the fairy, to protect her with his body. The witch screamed in pain, for her heart was broken. Her lover loved another more than her." She put her hands over her heart. "And she shrank and she shrank and she shrank. And as she did, the gnome sang a song. Can you guess what it is?"

"'Without Love You Are Nothing'?"

She groaned. "It's 'The Witch is Dead.' The fairy and the gnome watched her shrink until she was ant size, and still she shrank more."

"Isn't the fairy going to try to save the witch?" he asked. "Isn't that what fairies do?"

"You're confusing fairies with angels. In fact, to make sure the witch didn't come back, the fairy stepped on her. Crushing her under her silken slippers. And then, holding hands, she and the gnome ran together to the gnome house."

"This is the worst fairy tale I've heard."

"It's a fairy tale for adults."

"In that case, you'll tell me what happens in the gnome house."

"Aw." Her mouth curved down, and she gazed at him in sympathy. "You need instruction in that area?"

"I have a prurient interest."

"I'm not surprised. But that wasn't in our bargain. We'll end the story there."

They stared at each other, and it felt to him as if the air between them crackled with electricity.

"Doesn't this story have a moral?" he asked, and he heard a growl in his voice. The sound of a man with an erection.

"Sure, it does. 'Don't mess with fairies.'"

Staring at her, he said, "I don't plan to. I prefer real women."

"Funny. I thought you preferred witches." She stood. "I'm going to bed." Holding her head high, she strode out of the room.

He watched her disappear into the hall. Her leaving was a good thing, despite his hard-on. If there was a human equivalent of a fairy, she was it. And fairies could be tough.

But as he sat there, nursing his brandy, listening to the sounds of her brushing her teeth and getting ready for bed, the familiar nothingness draped over him like a shroud. It wasn't an emptiness from the outside but from the inside.

He'd been here over a week already. Her stories had filled him for a short time, but it made the time when she was away at work even emptier as he looked at the blank screen and sometimes keyed in words furiously with his two-fingered typing. But most often, he sat in front of the laptop, glaring at the screen, waiting for inspiration to strike him.

He finished the brandy and decided against another one. His drug was a woman, and he didn't need to add alcohol to that list of one. He got up and set the glass on the counter before heading upstairs.

He'd made his decision. Tomorrow, he would leave.

***

A warm weight on his head woke him up, and he made a noise, putting up his hands against a soft-furred animal that had decided to use his forehead as a pillow.

Ginger made a sound of indignation, which he took to be resentment that he dared to touch her. Apparently she shared the same attitude as her human. Then she stood and shook, as if she were shaking off his cooties. He closed his eyes to keep out falling cat hairs.

It was mid morning already, but he hadn't fallen asleep until early this morning. He got up, showered, dressed, and made his way downstairs with a good portion of the synapses in his brain still set on snooze. He needed coffee.

There was a note on the table, but first he used her fancy coffee machine to pour himself a cup of regular—something he would miss when he left, but he could buy his own—then he turned to the table to read the note.

My sister's having Thanksgiving at her house on Thursday. You're invited. I told her you'd come.

He looked at it for a long time. For so long that when he finally lifted his mug to his lips, the coffee was lukewarm.

It was probably because the sun was shining outside, and maybe it even had something to do with waking up with a cat on his head, or it might have been the note and his reluctance to be alone on a day when friends and family got together—though he doubted it, because for years holidays had meant just another day to him—but the emptiness he'd felt last night, and for so many other nights, no longer felt quite as empty.

Maybe he should stay. At least until after the holidays. See how Maddie acted with her sister and her sister's family. Watch them the way a primatologist in the wilds watched a band of gorillas.

It would be something he could use in a screenplay, because he sure the hell didn't believe in fairy tales.

12

This was a month of surprises. Maddie looked up at the two men heading into her office without knocking, as if they owned the place. In a sense, one did—bald-headed George Frickmann, the town administrator. Behind him was his son, with more hair, though it was receding. Some unlucky town in Minnesota had Duane as an administrator. Since he resembled his father in looks and actions, Maddie guessed that while he was visiting his family, some poor clerk in Minnesota was taking care of his administration duties—and she was probably taking care of his duties while he was there, too.

At least it wouldn't be long before George retired and she got paid more than twice as much for the work she was already doing.

So she smiled and stood to shake hands with Duane, who held hers a little too long, squeezing it and giving her a sleazy look.

She squeezed his hand back hard—and then harder—before dropping it like it was something yucky.

His eyes widened...and then he smiled, a glint in them. As if he'd liked the hard squeeze.

Ewww. She could've asked him about his wife and kids, but he wasn't worth it. Besides, slime had no discomfort level, so she turned to George. "I put some papers for you to sign on your desk."

He waved his hand at her. "No problem."

No problem for him. She kept her smile on, telling herself, *Soon he'll be gone from my office.*

They left, and she heard them in the front office with Caroline. About ten minutes later, Maddie's phone rang.

"Did you hear the news?" Caroline asked, her voice trembling slightly.

"About George? Is he leaving sooner?" He was slated to leave at the end of January, but his wife, Helen, had mentioned last week to Dolly at the Hair Place while getting her hair colored that she wanted to leave for Florida earlier. Dolly said they'd fought about it.

Maybe Helen had won that war. Maddie hoped so. The sooner George left, the sooner she would have his job and get more money to buy her new house.

"So you didn't hear." Caroline's lips twisted. She was a town native. Her husband had died of a massive heart attack when he was in his forties. "There's been rumors, but I didn't want to depress you."

Maddie frowned but didn't say anything. Usually she was up on all the rumors, but lately she'd been busy keeping her own secrets.

"You'd better come to the front," Caroline said, and this time there was no excitement in her voice. Just an "oh shit" tone.

***

It wasn't even break time, but the hell with it. Maddie was so furious she was surprised the snow didn't melt beneath her boots as she stomped up the sidewalk to Kevin Spindlebottom's real estate office that shared an old Victorian with the consignment store. Next door was the post office, and on the other side of that was the antique store.

But the only board member in this place was Kevin, and she marched into it, not caring if she left salt on his wooden floor and not wiping her boots on the doormat a hundred times like he preferred. Or better yet, taking off the boots.

As she burst into his office, he grabbed the phone that hadn't rung and put his hand over the receiver, as if covering it up so the caller wouldn't hear him talk to her.

His guilty expression was answer enough for her, his eyes darting away from hers. Nothing near the happy smile that had set off all the wrinkles in his face last week when she talked to him about finding a house. "This is an important call," he said in a stage whisper.

"No problem." She plopped down on the wooden chair in front of his desk. "I'll wait for you."

"It's private," he said.

"You can trust me. I won't say anything."

He stared at her with an admonitory frown. She stared back, and he must have gotten a clue from her fierce expression that she wasn't a happy dancer, because he said into the phone, "I'll call you back later, dear."

After setting the phone down, he folded his hands on the desk and leaned forward with a slight smile. "And how are you this morning?"

"George was in my office with his son. I found out that Duane lost his job in Minnesota."

Kevin shook his head. "A terrible thing when a man with a family loses a job."

"It's a terrible thing when a woman with a family loses one, too."

A muscle jumped in Kevin's cheek, and he leaned back, distancing himself a few inches more from her.

"You told me the job was mine. *Everyone* on the town board said I'd have the job."

He looked up and sighed heavily, his tensed shoulders sloping down. "Duane has experience."

"I stayed here five months after I got my master's on the promise that I would be the next town administrator."

He frowned and sucked in his lips. "It wasn't a written promise."

"I'm sure I have this in emails."

"That's not an official offer."

"Funny, I thought it was. And you and the other members seemed satisfied with it. Are you saying I shouldn't have trusted your word?"

His face flushed, his nose the color of the red wine he liked to drink. "That's not fair. Things changed."

"What hasn't changed is that I've been doing George's job for four years. I have experience."

"You've helped George. That's part of your job description."

She slapped her hand on his wooden desk. "The only thing George does is sign what I give him to sign."

Kevin's features tightened with distaste. "I'm sorry you feel that way, Maddie. Perhaps that's something you should have mentioned before."

"Perhaps I should have." She put her hands on her lap and curled them. "You have to vote on this, don't you?

Maybe not everyone will vote for him."

"Perhaps." Once again, his eyes evaded her, looking downward. And she knew that it was a done deal. That the board members had already discussed this on the phone or in a private meeting and decided what to do. When it came down to it, they were all natives…and she wasn't.

She stood. "First, I won't be looking for a house anymore. Second, I want the board to write down everything that is part of my job, so there won't be any overlap in the future. Is that a problem?" She glared at him, daring him to say it was a problem.

He shook his head quickly, leaning back farther. "No problem."

"I expect that list by the end of the week. Until then, I won't do any of George's work. Do you understand?"

He nodded.

"Good. Since you want everything in writing from now on, I'll type out a summary of our meeting as soon as I get back to the office and send a signed copy to everyone on the board."

Without saying good-bye, she stomped out, her boots thumping on the floor.

Coward. Well, screw him. Screw George. Screw the whole town board. Now that her workload was lightened by more than half, she had a lot of time to look for a new job.

***

Dog limped into the yard and lifted his head, but the

smell wasn't there anymore, the wind blowing the wrong way. He remembered the direction, but even if his leg was healed, he couldn't leave this place.

The girl needed him. At night, he slept in her bedroom. And while the sharp voices of her mom and dad knifed into the room, she lay on the rug next to him, pulled her covers off the bed and over both of them, then held on to him tightly. Sometimes her tears leaked onto his head before she fell asleep.

If he left her, who would she hold at night while she cried?

***

"What's wrong?" Logan asked. Dinner had been a salad and a mediocre frozen pizza. Maddie had been distracted, though she'd put on a good face for her son. But Logan had seen the unhappiness in her eyes and on her face. The way she stared at nothing.

Something had changed today, and the only thing he knew for sure by looking at her was that it wasn't a good change.

"Nothing's wrong." She settled down on the sofa with her glass of wine, ready to tell him her nightly story.

"You'd make a lousy actor." He frowned at her glass of wine. She'd used a regular glass, and she hadn't skimped.

That was one way to beat the blues, but not one he'd recommend for her.

"Good thing acting's not on my list of preferred occupations," she said.

"It might loosen you up a bit."

"So would a bottle of brandy."

"I know where you keep the brandy. Say the word, and I'll get it." He gave her what one interviewer had called his "wicked smile."

Going by Maddie's scowl, it didn't impress her. That normally would've made him smile wider, but not when she down was like this. "You can spend all night telling me nothing's wrong, and I won't believe you," he said. "I've got a radar about women's moods. And this mood of yours is seriously serious."

"Seriously serious? Isn't that redundant?"

"You're not going to distract me with a grammar question."

"I don't have to distract you. If I don't want to talk, I won't." She gave him her Ninja face. "And keep your radar to yourself. I'm here to tell you a story, not to be your daily optimist."

"If you were my daily optimist, you'd flunk. You're the least optimistic person I know."

"Not true. If I were a pessimist, I would've seen it... Never mind."

"You would've seen something coming," he said. "You practically told me what happened. If you won't finish it, I'll find out tomorrow."

"No, you won't. No one knows but me and one other person." Her voice was low and throbbed. She turned her head, hiding her expression from him. "And the town board."

"You're wrong. In a town this size, if that many people know, at least two-thirds of the town knows, too."

"You... You..." She set her lips together and looked out of the window.

"Man," he said, his voice lower than hers, as if it came from the pit of his belly. Or perhaps lower than that. "I'm a man."

"Are you?" She challenged him with her hard stare. "It feels to me you're more of a victim. Hiding out here with me and Zach. Hiding from a woman."

He stilled. For a second, he hated her.

She continued to glare at him, not saying anything. As if she wanted him to be angry at her. To hate her.

He leaned forward in his recliner. "Dexter told me this morning to call if I need anything. I know Dexter isn't as sharp as he used to be, but his wife seems to know everything that's going on in town. You don't have to tell me anything. All it will take is one phone call to Alma."

"I didn't know you were interested in gossip." Her voice was like a knife, and if her nose rose any higher, it would start bleeding. "If you're so interested, go ahead and call Alma. I doubt she knows."

"You want to put money on it?"

Her face closed up, all emotion hidden, but her shoulders slumped. "I'll pass. Call Alma. I don't care. You want to hear tonight's story or not?"

He wanted to say no, but he'd become addicted to her nightly stories. And maybe it would give him a clue as to what was happening to her. All her stories seemed to have a connection to her, each one a piece of the puzzle that made up her life. "Go for it."

"Once upon a time, there was a magician and a

witch."

"Another witch story."

"A good witch."

"It's so hard to tell the difference."

She stared at him, her eyebrows raised imperiously, until he sat back in his recliner, in listening mode. "Are you ready to let me continue?" she asked. "With no interruptions?"

"Yes to the first question. No to the second."

"I bet your teachers loved you."

He flashed her a smile. "I inspire either love or hate. No middle ground."

"I like the middle ground."

"I'm not surprised. The middle ground feels safe, doesn't it?"

"Not today. Okay, here's my story. There was a magician who really was a lousy magician. But he fooled a lot of people into thinking he was good. Because he *looked* like a magician. His father had been a magician before him, and he knew all the important people in the night clubs where he performed, and he wore all the right clothes. So they had no idea that he really had no magic tricks, and that he'd found a young witch who did all his tricks for him. And no one knew the difference."

"Why did the witch do that?" he asked.

"Because the magician was about to retire, and he'd promised her she could have his act when he quit." Her voice grew hard. "You can guess what happened next."

"He didn't quit."

"His son, who'd been a magician in a bigger city, lost his magician job. The magician broke his promise to the witch, giving his son the job instead. She could've found another job during this time, but she hadn't looked for one because of the promise. It was a bad time of the year, a time when there aren't a lot of jobs—"

"The end of the year, right?"

"Maybe." She shrugged, no expression on her face, just a dullness in her voice when she continued. "She told the magician she wasn't going to do his work anymore, and that meant she probably wasn't going to get a good recommendation from him." She made a face. "In fact, he'll probably do a lukewarm one, so he won't get sued. He's that kind of politician. I mean magician."

"They're all that kind of politician."

"Magician," she said in a firm voice that matched her closed expression. "But she's not sorry."

"Of course not. She's a woman of passion."

"She's a witch with a mean broom."

"I've always been partial to witches."

"I'm not surprised."

"So, what's the end of this story?" he asked. "Did she hex the magician? Did she put him under a spell that would make him give her a good recommendation? Or did she erase all the trick instructions from her computer?"

Her eyes narrowed, and she went still again. He couldn't hear her brain humming, but he could see it in the unseeing eyes with the occasional blink.

Then she frowned and inhaled, her nostrils flaring, a pained expression on her face, and her mouth twisted in a grimace.

"You're not going to do it, are you?" he asked.

"*She's* not going to do it. It would hurt...other people who depended on the magic acts she'd put together."

"A town full of people," he said, and she just stared at him. "And don't tell me this isn't about you. As a master liar, I can see right through you."

"That doesn't sound very comfortable. No wonder you're a cynic."

"Cynics aren't made, we're born. But this is about you, not me. I can get you a job in L.A. like that." He snapped his fingers.

"I don't know if I want to live in L.A."

"Where would you like to live?"

"A good place to raise Zach." One side of her lip lifted in a sad smile, no longer trying to fool him. As if she could. "A place where I can get a decent job. I feel like I'm back where I was five years ago." She shrugged. "This time I have some money, at least."

"And a GPS," he said.

"My phone comes with one."

"What about the town board? What do they say about the administrator electing his own son?"

"The town board hires the new administrator." Her forehead creased. "Kevin Spindlebottom from the board implied that it was a done deal. I'd noticed the other members avoided me lately, but I just thought they were too busy to talk."

"So-called friends tend to avoid you after stabbing you in the back."

"Or the heart." Slouching, she glanced down at her hands.

He got up from the recliner and stepped toward her.

Her head snapped up. She watched him, wary, like a cat watching a dog, as he sat on the ottoman, reached down, and picked up her right foot.

"What are you doing?" Her voice rose.

"Giving you a foot rub." He put her foot on his thigh. "Isn't that what you like? It was on your list."

She jerked her foot off his thigh. "I don't think—"

He grabbed her ankle and drew her foot back to her thigh. "Stop thinking and just relax." He held on firmly. Bending his head, he used the fingers of both his hands to massage her foot.

Her struggles ceased. He heard a sigh whisper through her, but he still was alert for any attempt to resist. After a few minutes, he felt the tension leave her leg. She closed her eyes, and her shoulders loosened.

"I was going to suggest we make love," he began, and her leg jerked back. He was ready for her, grasping it. "But I didn't think you'd go for it."

"You're right about that." Despite her leg jerk, her eyes were still closed, and the words came out dreamily.

"It would make you feel better."

"I've made love before, and to tell you the truth"—her voice was so sleepy he could hear a small slurring—"none of the times was as good as your massage right now."

"Then you had lousy lovers."

"Possibly." She raised her eyelids slightly and regarded him from beneath her lashes. "I'm sure you're going to tell me you're the exception."

He glanced upward even as he kept massaging. "Some things are better shown than told."

"Some things are better left to the imagination."

"You're imagining me making love to you?"

Her face flushed, and her leg pulled back. Once again, he was ready for this, holding her ankle. "Just relax. No more talking. Close your eyes. You know you want it."

"Pig." Her eyes closed, though. "I'm only doing this because I had a really bad day, and I need this."

"And I'm good at this."

Her eyes remained closed. "We already established that. How many times do you need to be told?"

"Never. I know how amazing I am."

She laughed softly, and the tension left her leg and foot again. Completely relaxed as he found all the pulse points, she rested her head against the back of the sofa, looking up at the ceiling.

He set her foot on the ottoman next to his hip, in contact with his jeans, then picked up her other foot and began to massage that. After a moment, he stripped off her sock. She made a sound of satisfaction. Glancing up, he saw she was gazing down at him, her eyes half-lidded as he massaged her foot.

"Just relax," he murmured. "I'm just rubbing your feet. That's all."

Her eyes closed again, and another languorous breath sighed through her. He rubbed her foot for a few minutes before he said anything.

"I wonder why he was let go from his job at the other town?"

13

She jerked her foot back, and this time he let her go. She angled forward on the sofa. "I never thought of that. I'll Google it."

He stood, the movement pushing the ottoman away from him. "I want to see this, too."

She was already moving away when he grasped her right arm beneath her elbow. She glanced back, and he dangled her sock in front of her. A sense of lightness made her laugh, her body still relaxed, like marshmallows pulled until they were stretched into taffy. She grabbed the sock and kept going, one foot warm and one foot cold. The same way she felt about Logan, warm and cold. Though right now, the warmth was winning.

It had been a lousy day, and the place she'd come to for refuge seemed to be turning its back on her.

But Logan had been there for her with a foot massage. The ultimate relaxant. The ultimate aphrodisiac.

He reached her netbook on the desk at the corner of the living room first. "Put on your sock. I'll Google."

"It's my computer."

"Don't worry. I know my way around a computer." He gave her a wicked grin, silently telling her that a computer wasn't the only thing he knew the way around.

It made her want to hit him. At the same time, his grin swept away the tension rising inside her, and she knew that was his intention to take her mind off what the town board had done.

She still might have argued, but it dawned on her, like a slap in the face, that he wanted to be seen as devilish, an old-fashioned rake, the bad boy. But in reality, he was a nice guy. All the evidence pointed to it. Keeping his grandmother's house for nearly a decade for sentimental reasons. Letting her and Zach stay—and not calling the sheriff. And now, trying to help her.

Sure, not all of his intentions were noble. If she suddenly gave into her lust and hopped into his bed, she was pretty sure he'd hop in with her. He certainly was no saint—but who was? Besides, she suspected that a saint wouldn't be nearly as interesting or fun. And a saint wouldn't make her feel...desirable and interesting and alive in every sense of the word. Bodily and emotionally.

He asked her Duane's name and the town he'd worked in then typed it in quickly for a man who only used two fingers on each hand. He hit enter then his fingers stilled, and he glanced up at her, two vertical lines between his eyebrows. "Something else is going on with you."

What? Did he sense her thoughts? "Nothing. Are you a mind reader?"

"It's my next profession." His eyes glittered, and he gave her his I'm-a-devil grin again. "Don't tell anyone, or the government will know I'm really an alien. That's the real reason I left L.A. One day I noticed there seemed to be a lot of men in black wherever I went, and I decided to get out while I could. All the stuff I told you about the dark queen was bullshit."

"No worries. Every time you tell me something, I suspect it's bullshit." She ignored his quick laugh and continued, her voice sharpening. "As for what's wrong, you tell me the deeper issues about your life, then I'll tell you mine. Until then, stop being so nosy, and let's find the dirt on Duane."

He narrowed his gaze at her. She raised her eyebrows and stared at him, unblinking, until he turned back to the screen. His face muscles tightened, and a frown etched on his forehead, his eyebrows slashing together as he clicked on one link and another. Finally, he swiveled on the chair.

"Nothing. All the other links are older and probably more obscure. None of them say anything damaging."

"He's kind of slimy," she said. "I bet he had an affair with someone and was caught."

Logan clicked onto the website of the town board where Duane had worked before. He nodded his chin at the image of Duane, still in the town board photos. "He looks like a former quarterback in high school, gone to fat. The kind of guy used to getting any girl he wants. I wouldn't be surprised if it was something sexual."

"Someone under eighteen. Or the wife or daughter of someone on the board."

"I hope so. Then they'll be more likely to talk."

"Talk to who?"

He just smiled, pushed back, and stood.

"*I* want to talk to them," she said.

"Better not. You might get in trouble."

"Are you hiring an investigator?"

He just smiled at her. "I'm going upstairs to write. I feel motivated."

"I didn't even tell you a story tonight. Not a real story.

I was spewing."

"Sweetheart..." He looked down at her as if she were his favorite ice cream and he wanted to eat her. "Holding your bare feet in my palms more than made up for it."

He strode away, leaving her staring at his back with her throat too tight to say anything without squeaking.

Damn him. He'd irritated her on purpose.

But there were a lot of men who were douches, and she was ninety-five percent sure he wasn't one of them.

It unsettled her. She'd feel...safer if he was one. She couldn't deny she was wildly attracted to him. She was human. Blood ran through her veins, and he was pretty to look at. He probably got hit on all the time. Probably by both sexes, though the way he oozed testosterone, she was ninety-nine point nine percent sure he was straight. The fact that he was turning out to be one of the good guys was just going to make it harder to say no to him.

None of it mattered. He was in love with one of the most beautiful women in the world, and any short affair she might have with him would not have a happy ending. Unlike him, she preferred happy endings in her fiction, and in her life. The next time she took that leap with a man, she needed to be sure that the guy she was leaping to would be there to catch her. And that man wasn't Logan.

***

In the bedroom upstairs, Logan stood at the window and looked out at the dim night and breathed deeply. Since Olivia had come to his house in Beverly Hills to tell him they were done, he'd felt numb. Only half alive.

That had slowly changed, starting the night he'd walked into his grandmother's house and found it occupied by the very prim, on the surface, Madelyn Barrymore. He'd quickly discovered she had depths and a few murky spots. Her audacity at living in his house for so long, mixed with her ferocity when her son was concerned and the way she'd helped others in town, had gotten to him that first night. Had awakened dormant senses.

Tonight he felt fully alive, all his senses stirred and awakened.

The unfortunate part was that he wanted to lie down with Maddie more than ever.

And he could tell by the way she darted looks at him and the flush in her cheeks that she wanted to lie down with him, too.

Naked.

Touching.

Kissing.

Licking.

Locking her legs around him.

Begging him to love her. Pleading. Until he finally said yes and eased his way into her.

She'd be tight, because it had been so long since she'd had sex. Her muscles would clasp him.

So would her arms.

She wouldn't want to let him go.

It would be ecstasy.

It would be—

A mrrrwl sounded, and something slashed his hand.

He snapped around and stared at the hissing cat. Then, as if nothing had happened, the cat turned and padded out. In no hurry. Her tail up in the air.

Looking down at the back of his hand, he saw four streaks of blood.

Jesus, did the cat really know what he was thinking?

Impossible. His hand stung, and he crossed to the bathroom to wash off the blood. The cat reminded him of too many women he knew back in L.A. Cute and deadly.

Move over, guard dogs, he thought, the guard kitties are vicious.

14

The tap of shoes on the floor gave Maddie a ten-second warning. Time enough to switch from the dating site on her computer to the office site. She twisted around in time to see Patty Kohlman from the town board stomp in. The years hadn't been good to the former beauty queen, but she didn't appear to give a damn. In her late-fifties, she wore no makeup, no hair dye, no high heels. What Maddie had appreciated most was her policy of no bullshit.

Until today. Patty sat heavily in the visitor's chair and looked Maddie straight in the eye. "I wanted to tell you earlier."

Maddie raised her eyebrows, not saying anything. She'd already found out that a lover could stab her in her back. Now she knew that people she'd considered her friends did the same thing.

Patty leaned forward. "Kevin said you were angry."

Maddie still didn't say anything.

"It's nothing personal."

"Really?" She couldn't hold back any longer. "It's personal to me."

"Duane is experienced."

"I've been doing the job of the town administrator for a good four years while George signed whatever papers I told him to. I'm pretty sure you all knew that. So I have more experience in this town, and I have the degree. Besides that, I was promised the job. *You* promised me the job, and so did the others."

"Things changed. Duane has a wife and two children."

"Good. Let him look for a job. With his experience, he should have no trouble, right?"

"You are angry."

"You're damn right I'm angry." Her voice rose, words spewing out, her control shattering. "I could've been looking for a job since August. The board asked me not to, telling me to hold on. And now you tell me that 'things changed.' This is ugly, and I feel that I've been taken advantage of. I think there could be some gender discrimination here, too."

Patty sat up stiffly. "Are you thinking of suing?"

"Am I?" She was shaking and hot, and tears weren't too far away. "I have a case. And betrayal is a bitch, isn't it?"

"Maddie, we've known Duane since he was a baby. I babysat for him. It would be a worse betrayal if we didn't help him. Please understand."

"I understand. You decided to betray me instead." She stood and pointed toward the door. "If you don't mind, I'm trying to get my work done. I don't think we have anything more to say."

Patty sighed, pushed out of the chair, and got to her feet. When she turned, her eyebrows shot up. "What are you doing here?"

Maddie swung around and saw Caroline standing in the doorway of the adjoining office, holding a handful of envelopes.

"I have mail for Maddie."

"How long have you been here?"

Caroline's eyes narrowed. She wasn't much younger than Patty, and she liked to say that she didn't take crap from anything. "Long enough."

Maddie's laugh was harsh to her own ears. "Thank you for stopping off today, Patty. I think I've got a witness."

Patty gave another sigh, and she shook her head. "I hate to see all this discord. I'll talk to the board, and we'll see what we can do."

Maddie pressed her lips together. She was shaking too much to say anything more. Patty's face scrunched together, as if she was as upset about this as Maddie. One more sigh, and she walked out of the office, past Caroline, and out the door.

Caroline followed her into the hall, and if Maddie wasn't so upset, she would have laughed at her for making sure the enemy was leaving the building. Finally, Caroline stepped back into the office. "She's gone."

Only then did Maddie plop down into the chair, her chest cold.

She'd thought she could trust Patty. Thought she could trust this town.

Once again, how stupid could she be?

Then Caroline's arms were around her, and it took a moment before Maddie could lift her arms and hug her back. Just one second, then she pulled away. She needed to get out of here.

***

Logan was on his phone in the kitchen when the cat

meowed loudly and dashed to the side hall. He stood, holding the phone to his ear. It was only late morning, and the cat was getting louder. He remembered his grandmother had mice once when he was young, and he wondered if Ginger had found one.

Instead, the door opened, and Maddie stepped in with her face too pale and her eyes too big.

"I've gotta go." He hung up on a screenwriter friend who was trying to talk him into reading his newest screenplay. "What the hell happened to you?"

She pulled off her hat then shrugged out of her jacket, tossed it on a hook in the hall. "Nothing. I'm taking a sick day."

"You have the flu or something?"

"Or something." She knelt to pet the cat, not meeting his eyes. "I've decided to use up some of my sick days."

"Bullshit. Something happened."

"I'm going to my room." She straightened then walked out of the kitchen, her head averted, still not looking at him.

He frowned, and his phone rang. He picked it up. His friend again, not ready to give up.

For the ten minutes that he talked to his friend, he listened for sounds from her bedroom. Finally, they hung up, and he headed for her room. The door was closed, and he knocked. "Are you okay?"

No one answered.

He was about to repeat his question then thought, what the hell, and opened the door. She was sitting on his grandmother's old rocking chair, wrapped in a blanket.

"You're sick," he said.

"No." She looked straight ahead. "I'm angry."

"This is how you act when you're angry? You don't throw things? You don't yell?"

"Patty, one of the board members, came to my office to talk to me today. I thought she was my friend."

"The kind of friend who comes with a sharp knife and waits for you to turn your back," he said. "I know those friends."

She shifted to look in his eyes with her sad ones. "She's afraid I'm going to sue them."

"You have grounds?"

"I printed out the emails from the board members telling me I had the job as soon as George retired in January. Maybe it wasn't a signed document, but I might have found another job during that time."

"Of course you saved them. You're Miss Efficient. They had to know that. They messed with the wrong woman."

"I don't think they know that." Her forehead creased. "But other people know about their promise. It wasn't a secret. And Patty affirmed it today with Caroline listening."

"You have a good case."

"I do." Her lips curved into an attempt at a smile that immediately curved down. "But I don't know if I'll sue."

"They shafted you."

"Yes, but I don't want to be like them. What happened today, me making Patty believe I might sue...that's what made me feel sick."

"They deserve it."

"I know."

"You feel like you can't trust anyone," he said. "That's it, isn't it? It's like a rock in your heart."

She looked at him, her expression flat, not saying anything.

"It's a common feeling where I come from. Happens all the time."

"If you're trying to cheer me, you're doing a horrible job."

He stared at her. Without any animation in her face, she looked miserable and almost plain, but he perversely wanted more than ever to hug her, to make her feel better. He sat on the edge of the bed and stroked his hand over her hair, from her top to the nape of her neck.

A spark glimmered in her eyes. "I'm not a cat."

"I know exactly what you are. I'm going to run a warm bath for you. You'll feel better." He got to his feet. "And I wouldn't do that to a cat."

"You're not doing it for me, either. If I want a bath, I can run my own water."

"Watch me." Before she could say anything more, he strode away.

***

She only took the bath because she didn't want to argue with him. Besides, baths were a luxury for her. Some mornings she was lucky if she had time to shower. And he'd gone to the trouble to find the lavender bath oil that probably had been pushed to the back of the cupboard below the sink. He must have gone on his knees on the hard tile to get it out.

And then he put on his CD with a man and a woman singing opera. *Opera.* In a language she didn't speak. That was crazy, and she didn't know why he'd done it, but she wasn't stepping out of the warm bath to turn it off. Especially since it sounded passionate and foreign, and she just knew that the singers had much worse problems than hers. So, she wasn't going to get the job she wanted. The job she deserved. So what?

She had Zach, the greatest kid in the world.

She had Ginger, who was a sweetheart.

She had money in the bank. All that money she'd saved to pay back the house's owner. Now she could use it to get her, Zach, and Ginger through the next few months until she found a new job.

And she expected to get a glowing reference from the board. So bright and brilliant anyone reading it would be crazy not to hire her.

And to top it off, she could've been in jail. Instead, she was telling one of the hottest men she'd ever met a story every night.

Put in this perspective, she was a lucky woman. Probably one of the luckiest in the world.

"You okay in there?" he asked.

Warm moisture welled up in her eyes, her tear ducts not believing in her luck.

Stupid, stupid, stupid. First she'd shut down her emotions. Now they were overwhelming her.

She'd gone through this before, the ups and downs that left her feeling raw, with all her nerves exposed. At least she was in the bathroom alone, and if she stayed in

the cooling tub long enough, no one—meaning Logan—
would know she was so emotional.

A knock came on the door, and she made a sound that
came out as "Erk!"

"You okay in there?" Concern thickened Logan's
voice.

She couldn't answer, a big glob of words stuck in her
throat now.

"I'm coming in."

"No," she said in a squeak, but the door was opening.
She put her arm over her breasts and drew her legs up.
"Get out."

Of course, he didn't listen. Instead he closed the door
behind him, stood in the bathroom, his gaze running
over her. Then he stepped forward, grabbed the towel
from the towel rack, and held it out to her. "Your water
must be cold."

"Your balls must be made of steel."

One corner of his lips curled up. "You're wrong.
They're flesh and blood. Anytime you want to feel them
to be sure, you just go ahead."

Despite the cooling water, she was feeling warm.
"Thanks for the invitation, but I'll pass."

"Today," he said. "Tomorrow you might feel
differently. The offer will still be open. Now take the
towel."

"It'll get wet."

"Then stand." His eyes crinkled. "I won't look down."

She stood then grabbed it from him, and his eyes
locked on hers. Not that it mattered if he looked down.
He'd probably seen hundreds of nude women's bodies.

Most of them probably more shapely than hers—possibly with some help, but she didn't judge them.

"I won't need your help getting out." She wrapped the towel around her and tucked one edge over the other to hold it together. To make sure it wouldn't slip, she held it above her left breast. She'd already exposed too much of herself to him.

"Better safe than sorry." He curled his hand around her upper arm.

"I didn't know you were so worried about safety." She stepped out of the bathtub. This was turning into a farce, but she was grateful to him for pulling her out of her funk. "I'm out now." Out and dripping onto the bath mat. "You can go."

"When we're having so much fun?" The skin around his eyes crinkled again. "And this is your sick day. I should stick around to make sure you won't get deathly ill."

If anyone asked her, she would swear the devil was in his eyes. And her raw emotions responded to the devil's call in them. He radiated sex, and she was more vulnerable than usual today, desire creeping under her skin, her blood flowing faster, her breaths faster, too. She wanted to tilt toward him, lean against him, say and do things she'd be sorry for later. But right now, she craved him badly.

"I'm burning up," she said. "You'd better go. This isn't a good idea."

He curved his hand over her shoulder, his brilliant blue eyes scorching her from the inside out. "Maybe you're right."

"I *am* right." Her voice was hoarse.

"But you know what the problem is?"

"You're a horn dog, and I'm an emotional wreck."

"My problem is..." His voice lowered to a whisper. "I don't care if it's good or bad, I only care that I want you."

"But you're the kind of man who wants every woman. You—"

His lips stopped hers. She stood still, expecting his kiss to be hard and demanding. Instead, his lips were warm and soft. A contrast to his body that pressed against the length of hers in jeans and a flannel shirt.

The kiss stayed soft. So soft that she was the one who pressed against him, teasing him with her tongue, wanting him with her hands on each side of his face, as if to make sure he didn't get away.

A plaintive meow came from the other side of the closed door. Ginger's let-me-in demand.

Maddie jerked back from Logan, her breaths puffing out and in too fast. Logan leaned in to her, and she lowered her hands on his chest to hold him away from her.

"We have to stop this," she said. She was like the Wicked Witch in "The Wonderful World of Oz." On the verge of being melted.

He stepped back, and she immediately missed him.

"Come into my bedroom," he said.

"Logan, it's—"

"Not what you think."

She wrapped her arms around her front, partially because her towel was slipping. "Then what is it?"

"A massage. It will relax you. No sex."

"Promise?" Immediately she held out one hand, the other holding the towel up. "No, don't promise anything. I've already had too many promises broken."

"I promise it will make you feel good. It will relax you." He said it without a smile, and his eyes burned into hers. "That's my promise."

She had to hold back a moan. She loved massages; they were the present she gave herself and her sister for Christmas. Their feel-good-together gift.

He crooked his finger at her. "Come." Then he turned and headed out of the bathroom to his bedroom.

She padded after him, as if an invisible string were attached to her, pulling her toward his bed.

15

She insisted on putting towels over his sheets and the pillow to keep them from being saturated with the almond oil he'd found in the bathroom. When the bed was covered to her satisfaction, she lay down on her stomach, the tension visibly returned to her back. He could see the tautness of her muscles.

He was taut, too. But it wouldn't be the first time, and he could ignore it.

All of this rushed through his mind while he dribbled almond oil onto his hands. He was about to start the massage when she pushed up from her waist, holding the towel against her chest and twisting to look at him.

"Did you turn up the heat?" Her tone was accusatory.

"You can't get a massage in a cold house. Don't worry about the bills. I'm paying for them."

"No, you aren't. I had the bills transferred to my name after I moved in." Color flushed her cheeks. "Well, as soon as I started to make money." Her eyebrows contracted. "And stop staring at me like that."

"How am I staring?"

"As if you're a werewolf, and you want to take a bite out of me."

He laughed low in his throat. "I don't bite, just nibble. And I was just thinking how adorable you are."

"Of course. That's what men always think when they see me half naked."

"You're afraid. That's what this is about. Don't worry.

I've been told I'm as good at this as a professional."

She narrowed her eyes at him suspiciously, and he wouldn't have been surprised if she was still mulling over the heating bill. But she finally lay down, her back to him, her head cradled on her forearm.

He sat on the side of the same cherry wood bed his father had been conceived on. Not a good thought right now, so he banished it, easy to do as he put his hands on her back and felt her small shudder. A shudder of delight, he told himself, because it made him feel good to believe it. And for too long he'd been feeling bad.

He started with her neck, digging his fingers into her tense muscles.

"That hurts," she said.

"Told you I was giving you a real massage and not a seduction." He stilled his fingers and bent to whisper in her ear. "Disappointed? I can do the other choice."

She shivered and shook her head. "This is fine."

He slanted up and dug in again. He'd thought that's what she would say so wasn't disappointed. But if she'd admitted she wanted him, he would have obliged her. Happily. Eagerly.

He wanted her. He'd wanted her from the first day, when he'd walked in with a dead heart and found her occupying his grandmother's house, like one of the characters in the stories she was telling him.

His heart may have been dead, but his body was still alive. If she'd been a grasping phony, like so many of the women he knew, he wouldn't feel this way about her. But she was earnest and kind and all the things that he'd ignored in his previous life. And after months when nothing had seemed funny, she made him laugh.

But he wasn't laughing now, his attention focused on her tight skin and tighter muscles. As he worked his fingers over her neck muscles, they loosened, and he gentled his strokes. She gave a small moan, and he moved on to her shoulder muscles, pressing down hard.

She groaned, a big difference from a moan, which was good, because he wasn't made of stone. He was a selfish man, a horn dog, just like she'd said, but for this one time, he was being unselfish. For this one time, he wanted to do this for her. He wanted to heal her body, to help her heal her emotions from the blow of betrayal.

"You're slowing," she said.

"Some things aren't meant to be fast."

"Do you have to make everything sexual?"

"I didn't know I was." He grinned. "Maybe it's not me. Maybe it's you."

"Ha!" But she lowered her head, and he kept up the slower and gentler massage. The worst of the tension had been rubbed out of her shoulders and neck, and her other muscles were loosened. She was more relaxed, breathing easier.

Finally, he sat up. He wasn't used to giving deep muscle massages, and his hands felt the stress. "You can turn over," he said.

She didn't move, lying with her head to the side on his pillow, completely relaxed. He bent and saw her eyes were closed. Her breaths were shallow and soft. Her mouth parted, as if for a kiss. But he saw it was in sleep.

He watched her while he tried to figure out what it was about her that made him like her so much. Maybe her desire to do right by her son and by him, and by all the people she'd helped—even if she helped them by letting them into his home without his permission.

Though he wouldn't tell her, he admired her for not asking permission—which he wouldn't have given. He admired her proactivity.

Hell, why twist himself into a corner with reasons? He just admired her. He just liked her. He just wanted her.

And right now, he wanted to do something else he'd missed for a long time.

He took off his jeans, slung them at the chair in the corner, not caring that they missed and slumped to the floor. Then he laid on the bed next to her, barely an inch away, close enough to feel her heat. He drew the covers over both of them.

Closing his eyes, he relaxed, feeling the fog of sleep ready to take him away. But something was different about the fog tonight. It was...a happy fog.

A pounce onto his pillow stopped his thoughts, then a warm weight pressed against the top of his head.

The cat. Logan breathed evenly, too relaxed to move as sluggishness dragged at the dark corners in his darker mind and, in the deepening half sleep, he inched closer, pressing himself against her side.

***

Something was pressing against Maddie's hip. A hose? In a fog of sleep, Maddie shifted, but the hose followed her, and it was too much trouble to get away from it. But the pressure was tugging her from her dream where she'd just fired everyone on the board. Maybe waking was good, because she was feeling sorry for the board members.

Sorry? Really? After what they'd done to her?

Her half-dream, half-awake emotions flared in conflict. They should pay. They should suffer. They deserved it.

But she didn't want to watch or listen to their petty arguments. She didn't even want to think about it. She just wanted them to play nice with her.

She shifted again, and the hose pressed harder. A sound accompanied it, a moan. A masculine moan.

Her eyelids snapped open. Memory snapped back.

Logan. She felt the heat coming off him, that side warmer than her other side.

But nowhere as warm as her insides.

He'd been there for her last night. This man she'd only known a couple of weeks. This man who was in love with another woman.

She jerked away from him. The clock at the bedside told her she'd slept for almost an hour. Napping during the day was normally a luxury for her. She rolled to her side, facing Logan. His eyes opened, and they looked different, a darker blue. A frown formed between his eyes, and he looked young, though he was older than her by a half dozen years. But even more upsetting, this man who was always so confident looked...bewildered.

With a sigh, she reached up and rested her hand on his shoulder. His skin felt as warm as if he'd been sunbathing on a beach in Spain for an hour. No wonder she'd felt his heat.

"Hey," she said. "Were you awake all that time?"

"I just woke up." His voice reverberated outside her and inside her. His voice alone made her want to melt against him like butter on warm toast.

And then there was the rest of him....

Most of all, there was his kindness.

Of everything that attracted her to him, everything that made her soft, that made her want to lean in and kiss him, his kindness was the biggest.

"A part of you was already awake," she said. "I felt it against my hip."

His lips quirked. "That part is always at least half awake."

"Really? I thought penises were a lot like snakes, and even snakes sleep."

"Snakes?" The corners of his lips curled higher. "You haven't had sex in a long time, have you?"

"Since I left Chicago."

"Five years?"

She nodded.

"He must've been a lousy lover for you to stop doing something that feels so wonderful."

An ache grew in her. She'd had three lovers in her life. Sex had been...okay.

She wanted more. She wanted amazing.

"Show me," she murmured, her voice shaking only a little.

"Show you what?"

She slid her hand around his shoulder. "How wonderful it can be."

He stilled, his eyes sharpened, watching her the way he'd watch an injured bird that any second might flap its wings and fly away. "You're sure?"

"Are you going to try to talk me out of it?"

"What do you think?" He shifted closer to her, his arm curving around her back. The cotton of his T-shirt came into contact with her bare breasts, and she realized the towel must have slid off of her while she slept. Yet he hadn't leered. Hadn't even glanced down.

Why should he? They were just breasts, and he'd probably seen his share. More than his share.

He stopped a breath away from her lips. "You're thinking too much. I can see it in your eyes."

"I'm not thinking about you."

Smile lines rayed out from the corners of his eyes. "If you think that's flattering, you're wrong."

"I was thinking of all the women in Europe who sunbathe topless."

"None more beautiful than you."

She raised her eyebrows. What about your dark queen? she thought, but didn't ask. She didn't want to bring the other woman into bed with them. "It doesn't matter who's more beautiful or not. I'm in bed with you right now. Just this one time, I want to…"

"Be wild?"

She shook her head. "To know what it's like to be well loved."

He brushed a finger down the side of her face, tracing her cheekbone. "I should try to talk you out of it."

"Why?"

"If this were a movie, that's what the hero would do."

141

"I don't want a hero, I want a lover."

"In that case, we need to stop talking and start kissing." Then his lips were on hers, and she kept her eyes open for a second, but his were closed and his lips open, while hers were the opposite.

Maybe her mind had forgotten how to do this, but her body's memory kicked in, and her eyelids lowered, a sigh shivered through her body, her lips parted, and she melted against him. He still wore his T-shirt, and the cotton was soft against her skin and her nipples. Eyes still closed, she ran her hands down his sides, feeling his ribs beneath, and the lean muscles.

A moan came out of her. He'd removed his lips from hers to drop small kisses on her jaw, but now he moved back up to her lips, swallowing her next moan.

Her body heated and melted, and between her legs, she throbbed, and she wanted this, and she wanted some more. A whole lot more.

"I'm taking advantage of you." He pushed up from her. "This is an emotional time for you. You're needier than ever."

She shook her head. He didn't know, because she hid it too well, but she'd always been needy. She'd always craved love and approval. She'd thought maybe most people did. But this... What she was doing now...

"If that were true, I'd be doing this with any man."

"Any man who happens to be sleeping in your bed."

She lifted her hand, and it felt heavy, weighted with passion. "I wouldn't allow any other man this close to me. Stop trying to make me change my mind." She frowned and pulled back. "Unless you're having second thoughts."

He pressed against her, his erection unmistakable. "Right now, I can barely think at all. I'm just feeling."

"Then shut up and make love to me."

His chuckle rumbled out. She closed her eyes because looking at him was dazzling her senses, and she just wanted to feel. Feel his hands on her, feel his kisses and then his nibbles. Just like he was doing now. Wonderful touches, kisses, and nibbles.

And she touched, kissed, and nibbled back.

Their breaths turned harsh, and her body heated. She threw off the heavy quilt.

"I'm going to make a meal out of you," he murmured, moving lower. And then he found a spot to nibble on that made her cry out and clutch his shoulders.

"A fast meal," she said, her voice strained because this was so wonderful.

But he didn't listen to her. Not going fast but slow. All she wanted to do was cry out and cry out and cry out. Over and over and over. And more and more and more. Until finally, she slumped back as tremors shuddered through her body. Each one a tiny bit less, until finally she was done.

And then he moved between her legs, his erection nudging against her. He slid inside her slowly, and as if that turned on a switch, tremors shuddered through her again. Delicious tremors. She held on tight and cried out, again and again and again. As if her body were making up for five years of abstinence. Her legs folded around his thighs, her arms curved around his back. As he made love to her, he kissed her deeply. Then he raised his head, cords standing out in his neck, his face looking tortured as he shouted out wordlessly.

It seemed to go on forever before he collapsed on top of her, both of them warm and sweaty. They stayed like that for moments, the shudders in their bodies easing, their breaths slowing, their pounding hearts quieting.

He lifted his head, and she smiled at him.

"I made you smile." His voice was hoarse, his eyes gleaming. "I guess I've done my job well."

"I was just thinking that it would be easy to kill a man at a time like this, when he's so vulnerable."

Laughter lit up his eyes and his face, and she felt a different kind of warmth than a second ago. That warmth had started in her sex. This was in her chest. In her heart.

Way more dangerous.

That's when she realized he might hurt her in a different way than Zach's father had hurt her. She'd only known Logan for two weeks, but when they parted—because they would sometime—her life would be duller, flatter, darker.

She shivered and suddenly felt cold.

He slid out of her, and she felt the warm liquid in her. She stared into his eyes, horror whipping through her.

His lip curved down on side. "Looks like I forgot something."

"I didn't think of it."

"First time it happened to me."

"With…" She had to think of his name. "Todd, Zach's father, his condom broke. It wasn't anything I planned then or now."

He put his hand over her hair and brushed it back. "I know you wouldn't do that. It was my fault. And if you are pregnant, I'll love our baby."

She turned her head away from his hand on her hair. "I need to use the bathroom."

He didn't say anything for a moment then pushed away from her, rolling onto the side of the bed.

She scrambled off the other side. The towel was at the edge, and she grabbed it.

As she hurried away, thoughts jumbled inside her mind, good and bad and horrible and ecstatic. An overload of emotions, just because he'd said he'd love their baby. If he'd been angry or anxious, she would have shut off her emotions. But this...it squeezed her heart and sent tears welling up in her eyes.

In the bathroom, she turned on the shower, and though she'd taken a bath already, she stepped inside it and let the warm water pummel her as her warm tears trickled down her face. Finally the tears stopped, and she grabbed the towel off the towel rack and wrapped it around her.

When she stepped out, he was standing there, his clothes on.

"It's like déjà vu," she said. "You in the bathroom with me."

"I could get addicted to this easily."

"So could I." She gazed up into his blue eyes, as beautiful as everything else about him. "That's why we need to stop it now."

"I wanted you to know I meant what I said. Whatever happens, I won't be sorry. I would love our child."

The words "love" and "our child" shimmered through her, and she wrapped the towel tighter around her. "I know you would." She looked down finally, her eyes heating with tears again. She would not cry, she told herself. She would not.

Instead of leaving, he moved closer, his hands cupping her upper arms. "I won't leave you."

She raised her chin, fierceness pouring through her. She would not be an object of pity. "You're in love with another woman. I wouldn't want you around."

His head snapped up. He let go of her arms and stepped back.

"I don't need a man," she said. Not if she and her baby were just a responsibility.

She wanted more than that.

"Just my money." Gruffness edged his voice.

"I don't even need that. Not if I can make my own." She put a hand to her forehead, still holding the towel up with her other hand. "If I'm pregnant—and that's a big *if*—of course I'll want you to be a part of his or her life." Her voice thickened, and tears moistened her eyes. She blinked and kept on going. "And Zach's life, too, because I can see how attached to you he is already. But you should know that I don't expect anything more. Or even want it. Unless two people love each other, they shouldn't be a family. Being married is a hard thing. And in our case, it would be an impossible thing."

He didn't reply immediately. The warm air from the shower was cooling, and her shoulders and arms were chilled. She told herself if he didn't leave in another moment, she would—

"I didn't want what happened to end like that," he said, his voice low.

"I was there, too."

"I've wanted you from the first morning I walked into the house."

She stood still, her heart thundering in her head. "Lust at first sight?"

"Lust at first conversation." The corners of his lips kicked up. "I got a kick out of the way you stood up to me. You made me laugh. That's a turn-on."

The thunder subdued. Or course it wasn't *love* at first sight. Not for either of them. She hadn't really expected him to say it. "I'll search the Internet and make a list of jokes."

"There you are again. No one talks to me like you do. You are the most down-to-earth person I know. And you're a great mom." He stopped. "But you wanted me to leave."

"Not yet. Go on." She was softening, but sometimes soft was good. This would be something for her to remember long after she was gone. "Tell me more wonderful things about me."

His eyes lit. "You're amazing in bed."

"To be honest, *you* were amazing in bed."

"It's true. I am."

She laughed and held the towel tighter. "I could be, too. I just need more practice."

"Um—"

"Not with you, of course." She spoke quickly, not wanting him to think she expected him to stick around. "Because we shouldn't do this again. But next time I have sex with a man, I think I'll need to be more active." She smiled at him, as if she didn't ache inside.

It was okay. This ache wouldn't last. He was just a man who'd dropped into her life a short time ago. An amazing man, but he would soon walk out again. And she would soon be out of this house, too. Probably out of the town. The odds were against her being pregnant. Odds favored her never seeing him again.

So she looked into his eyes and didn't let any of her thoughts of emotions show on her face, just the smile and the mischief. And he smiled back, shaking his head and looking at her with affection and admiration—and why shouldn't he? She was giving him an easy out.

And he was taking it, backing up a step.

"You're making it hard, talking about honing your skills with another man." He took another step back.

She couldn't think of anything snappy to say, so she just kept her smile on and her eyebrows raised, as if she were waiting for him to leave and was too sophisticated to say anything.

Time stretched as he nodded and finally left. As soon as the door closed behind him, she allowed her body to sag and tears to prickle her eyes.

Damn it, she wasn't going to cry over him.

She didn't love him. She *couldn't* love him. She'd known him for too short of a time, he wasn't even her type, and he was in love with another woman.

But the tears came anyway, and so did the truth that she couldn't deny. For whatever reason, the wrong man for her seemed to be the one she wanted.

This was awful, and she could never let him know.

16

A small, short-haired dog yapped as Logan followed Maddie into the one-story house that looked like it was three decades old. The TV was on, and the house smelled of baked turkey. A lanky man wearing a Green Bay Packers sweatshirt greeted Maddie and Zach. He set Maddie's apple pie on a side table in the living room then took jackets and scarves, talking over the dog barks. Zach unencumbered himself first and dashed off to play with a taller girl and a boy who looked about the same age as him, the dog chasing after him. All three of the kids seemed to be talking at once, and now that the dog was silent, Maddie introduced him to her brother-in-law, Cody, who told him that his job today was to keep the kids out of the kitchen until dinner was ready, and did he want anything to drink?

Before Logan could reply, an attractive, plumpish woman who bore a resemblance to Maddie barreled into the room. "I thought I heard you." She stopped and looked him up then down. "Wow, you're even prettier in person than on Google."

"Mom!" the girl said.

The boy slapped his hands over his mouth to hold back giggles. Zach frowned at Logan, apparently not liking the idea that his aunt found him good-looking.

Neither Maddie nor Cody blinked. "I told you he wasn't bad-looking," Maddie said, deadpan.

"She said a lot more than that." Kris winked at him.

"Oh?" He looked at Maddie, who smiled coolly at him.

He felt the chill. Yesterday had changed everything.

He wasn't sorry for what had happened, but he was sorry for the way she was wary of him now.

Hell, if their positions were changed—if he were a woman who'd had unprotected sex with a man—he'd be wary, too.

But she'd been right to call him a horn dog. If the chance came to make love to her again, he'd be humping her in a second.

He'd been around the rich, famous, and sometimes depraved for a good ten years. He thought of himself as sophisticated, but when it came to sex, he rutted like any other man.

"Hey, woman," Cody called, "why aren't you in the kitchen doing a woman's job? Bring us a beer while you're at it."

"Of course, darling." Kris fluttered her eyelashes at him. "Where do you want me to give it to you? Over your head or inside your pants?"

Zach and the other boy laughed, rolling on the carpet. The girl rolled her eyes but giggled.

Logan grinned. "So far, this is the best dinner party I've been to in years."

***

"I like him," Kris said. She and Maddie sat at the kitchen table, with the extra leaf put away now, and the kitchen cleaned up. The dishwasher was humming, and Maddie was succumbing to a turkey and pie coma. At least she'd been smart enough this morning to wear stretch jeans. She needed that extra give.

"Of course you like him." Maddie shrugged one shoulder because she was too zonked out to shrug both. "Like you said earlier, he's pretty."

"Cody and the kids liked him, too. And he laughed at things I said. Not everyone gets my humor."

Maddie opened her eyes wide. "Really? That's so hard to believe."

"Very funny." Kris leaned forward to slug her, and Maddie easily dodged her knuckles. Kris, a sugar addict, had eaten two pieces of pie and a huge serving of her sweet potato casserole that was so sweet it may as well have been a dessert. Whatever coma Maddie was in, Kris's was doubled.

"So what's going on between you two?" Kris asked. "I saw sparks. Lots of sparks."

"He's in love with someone else."

"He told you this?"

Maddie nodded then made a face. "He didn't mention love. He talks about being under her spell or enthralled by her. He calls her the dark queen."

Kris made a face, too. "The dark queen? Ick."

"I know."

"He's kind of dramatic, isn't he?"

"Not most of the time. Not really." She almost wished he were more dramatic. Then the thought of him caring about another woman wouldn't hurt.

"Well." Kris's lips pressed together. "I don't like him as much anymore."

"I'm sure Cody will be relieved. You really need to

watch your drooling."

"Ha! You should see him stare at the Victoria's Secret angels. Next time there's a commercial, I'll dump a tray of ice over his head to cool him down."

"He knows they don't look like that in real life, doesn't he?"

"He's in denial."

"I don't blame him. I'm in denial about a lot of things that are going around, too. Let's talk about something else."

"Okay. What's with your job?"

Maddie made another face and put her hands on her belly that was bigger than when she'd walked into the house. "Let's not talk about that now."

"You should talk to a lawyer. You can file a discrimination suit against them."

"They were my friends." Her heavy tone matched the feeling on her chest, as if a wrecking ball rested on it.

Kris's forehead creased. "Not real friends. If they were your real friends, they wouldn't have thrown you from the curb into the freeway."

"The freeway?"

A chorus of "oohs" and "icks" came from the living room, but Kris ignored the noise. "During rush-hour traffic, too."

"I know you're right, but I guess I'm more hurt than angry."

"Bastards. And you're too..." Her gaze flicked over Maddie, a quick gaze that saw everything.

"Don't say 'nice,'" she said.

"I was going to say wimpy." Kris peered over

Maddie's head. "What would you say?"

"Obviously you're the smart sister." Logan strolled to the table. "When someone bites you, you bite 'em back."

"You're my kind of guy." Kris batted her eyes at him. "If I ever divorce Cody, can I call you?"

"The second you sign the papers."

Kris grinned and turned to Maddie. "I like him."

"That's because you're shallow."

"He didn't arrest you. That's a point in his favor. And he's still letting you stay at his house."

"I know. But if you're too nice to them, they turn on you."

"There you go. You should've been bitchier at work."

"You should've shown them your true colors," Logan said.

"I agree," Kris said. "Let me file the suit for you. I'm sure I can still forge your signature. And I've got all the dirt."

"You're a credit to our family. I'm very proud of you." Maddie turned to Logan. "Why are you here? To mock me?"

"It's not always about you."

Kris laughed, and Logan turned to her. "I volunteered to give you the news about your dog. He puked on your living room carpet."

"Oh no." She groaned then lowered her head at Maddie. "You see what happens when you're too good to them?"

"What?" Maddie asked. "They eat too much and throw up?"

"Exactly." Kris stood. Two minutes later, she was

heading to the living room with cleaning supplies and a scowl. Logan took her place.

"I like your sister and her family."

"I got lucky with her." She smiled at him. It was...*nice* to sit here and talk to him with their stomachs full and feeling a little sleepy and a lot happy. She had things to worry about—but not now.

"You deserve some luck. And she's right. You should sue the town."

She shut her eyes then opened them. "I don't want to have this conversation."

"It's something you need to think about."

"I know, but I was hoping for a respite." She shrugged. The board members were probably phoning each other about her today instead of enjoying themselves with their families. "Maybe I should sue, but I won't."

"You still think they're your friends?"

"No." She looked at him then down at her hands clutched on her lap. "But I don't want that poison in me."

"What about Logan's dad? Did you ever search for him?"

Her stomach muscles tightened, and she shook her head.

"He might be a rich man by now. Doesn't Zach deserve his support?"

She turned away from him then back. "Yes, he does."

"But you never looked for him."

"He didn't deserve Zach." Her body was hot and not in a good way, with her stomach twisting.

"And you could've found a job in another town—or

anyplace. Because of the board's promise, you stayed at Angel Lake. You're not just hurting yourself financially, you're hurting Zach."

"I know."

"But you still don't want to sue them?"

She crossed her arms over her belly and bent forward in her chair. "I feel sick. I ate too much. Just..." She looked up at him and hated the surprise in his face. "Go away. Just go away."

"I'm back. I—" Kris stood in the entranceway. At her words, Logan turned to her, and Kris looked from Logan to her then back to Logan again.

"What did you say to her?" Kris demanded.

"I'm wondering why she's letting the town board walk over her."

Kris drew herself up to her whole five-four height, managing to look formidable. "That's none of your damn business. You're upsetting my sister, and I'm asking you nicely to leave my kitchen."

He stood slowly, staring down at Maddie. "It wasn't my intent to distress you."

She looked away from him. There was nothing to say. She disappointed him. She'd heard it in his words and seen it in his eyes. He'd admired her for being smart and funny and brave, and now he knew she was a fake. A coward.

As he walked away, Kris stood in front of her and leaned down.

"I'll never forgive Mom for what she did to you," she said. "Never."

Maddie glanced up and saw Logan in the entranceway

about four feet behind Kris. He was staring at them. He held her gaze for a moment then turned, leaving as Kris knelt and hugged her.

Laying her head on Kris's shoulder, Maddie put her arm around her back and held on tightly.

***

Maddie checked to make sure Zach was asleep before she made her way slowly upstairs. Logan had said he was passing on a story from her tonight. That after all the food, he would fall asleep before she was half finished.

He was a good liar, she gave him that. He'd eaten more than usual—they all had—but she knew the real reason.

His door was open, and she stepped inside.

"You won't let it go," she said, "will you?"

He was sprawled on the bed on his back, one leg bent. He still had on the blue cable knit sweater and jeans he'd worn to her sister's. He set down the pages he was reading. It could've been a script or a manuscript. She didn't know and didn't care.

His face looked sad, but not for himself, she thought. For her.

She hated it.

"I'm used to women coming to my room," he said. "But I admit I hadn't expected you to want more of me so soon."

"And you're so wonderful in bed," she said, raising her eyebrows.

"That's what they tell me."

She sat on the foot of his bed. She'd already slipped into her red-and-green-flannel pants—mostly because of the elastic waist—and she'd exchanged her purple sweater for a red sweatshirt.

"I see you dressed for seduction," he said.

"I hear they're Santa's favorite colors. You never know when he might drop by."

He grinned then his mouth turned sober. She tensed. She'd come here to talk...but on her time, not his. She wanted to go into this gently, not in an angry rush.

Why couldn't he just lie there and say nothing?

"I don't get you," he said. "You're brave and fearless when you're talking to me. But when the board screws you over, you back off, not willing to fight for yourself." He leaned toward her. "What did your mother do to you?"

She looked down at her crossed legs. Like it or not, this was it. "I was twelve when my parents split up," she said, beginning at the time when the change started, like all good stories—and sometimes the awful ones. "A month later, we were living with the man my mother later married. That was in Tennessee. My dad had been stationed there, but he was reassigned to Florida." She shrugged. "I think he requested the move. Kris was in high school already, and she elected to stay with my dad's mother in Chicago. My stepfather..." She stopped and swallowed.

"He abused you?" His tone was rough.

"No, not that." She shuddered. "I was moody and cried a lot and didn't like him. I guessed he and my mom were having an affair while she was still with my dad. I was mad at my mom for ruining our home, and I blamed my stepdad, too. For the most part, he ignored me, and sometimes he yelled at me. My friend's girlfriend told her mother, and her mother talked to someone at school. They called my mother in." Her voice choked up. All these years later, and her throat tightened up to talk about it.

"She didn't like being called in," Logan said, filling in the spaces. "She was angry."

"If you can imagine ice being angry, that was my mother. The next day, she packed a suitcase, drove me to the airport, gave me a ticket she'd bought online, and told me she was sending me to my father."

"Shit. What did your father say?"

"He cried and hugged me. He's a good guy. He didn't marry again for four years. I like my stepmother. I only left after they had twins because they were talking about moving to Alaska, and I wanted to be with my sister. I was almost eighteen then, old enough to leave home."

"Is that why you took in everyone who needed a helping hand? Why you let them stay here?"

Catching herself raising her shoulders defensively, she dropped them. "I don't analyze everything I do."

"You knew what they were going through."

"I did it because it was the right thing to do. I did it because, for this short time, I could help someone else who was desperate and going through a bad time. So mostly, I did it because I could." She could hear the hoarseness in her voice and knew he did, too. He didn't miss much. She glared at him. "Don't make a martyr out of me. Or a saint."

"When I look at you," he said, and his blue eyes turned hot, "I can guarantee you that I don't see a saint."

"Pig."

"I'm a man. Men are pigs." He held out his arms. "Come here."

"No." She pushed off the bed and stood. "I just came up because I knew you wouldn't stop until you found out. It's a stupid story, and you'd think I would've gotten over it by now."

"Your mother rejected you." He slid out of the bed, too. "She was a bitch, and when you acted up, she kicked you out. Now I understand."

"When you put it like that, I see it was...not a cool thing for her to do."

"You should write her a letter."

"A waste of paper. She'd crumple it up and throw it away."

He stepped toward her, and she backed up, stepping on something, a discarded shoe, she thought. Teetering, she waved her arms at her sides and said, "Ack." He took two long steps, slung his arm around her, and held her against him.

She closed her eyes and allowed herself to lean against him. "Stay with me," he murmured in her ear.

Her head snapped up. "I can't. Zach—"

"Zach is sleeping. You don't need to stay all night. Just for a while."

"It's a terrible idea."

He stepped back, taking her with him. "No talking. We won't say anything. I'll just hold you. Pretend I'm a teddy bear."

Laughing shakily, she drew away from his chest, but his arms around her back stopped her from moving farther. If she pushed at him and insisted, she was sure he would let her go. But she wasn't that angry. She wasn't scared, either.

And his arms around her felt...good. What would it hurt if she let him hold her for just another minute?

"Don't you trust yourself around me?" he asked.

Her eyebrows rose. "Really? You're daring me?"

He grinned. "I am."

Her heart beat faster. "You can't touch me sexually."

"It works both ways. You can't touch me sexually."

"Real funny." She fought to keep her lips from turning up.

"That sounds like a yes to me." Before she could say anything, he slid an arm behind her thighs and one behind her back then swept her up, like a man carrying his bride—and she didn't know why that analogy popped into her mind.

Instinct had her swinging her arms up to hold on to him and make sure he wouldn't drop her onto the floor. But his grasp was firm, and his arms were muscled. In seconds, he lowered her to the bed.

She stared up at him. "You're not soft enough to be a teddy bear."

"If I keep eating the way I did today, that will be fixed soon. After all the turkey, stuffing, and pie, I feel like a slug."

She looked him up and down again. Openly. Feeling...healed in a small way. A way that would let her lie on his bed instead of curling up into a ball of misery on hers.

"Like what you see?" The blue in his eyes darkened, and he smelled like sex.

"You know what you look like," she said, hearing the flatness of her voice when she felt anything but flat. Not at this moment. Not at any moment she'd been with him or near him or breathing the same air with him.

"You know, too. You saw me yesterday. All of me."

Her face heated. "I really wasn't paying attention to the way you looked." She'd noticed, though. Of course she had. In between the kissing, the touching, the sliding, the feeling, the heat, the orgasms.

Chuckling, he lay down next to her, his arm touching the length of her arms, his hips and legs touching hers.

It was like cuddling up to a warm oven. The only thing she missed was that he wasn't holding her.

She shifted to the other side of the bed, her face to the wall.

He shifted after her. "You're hard to figure out."

"I'm the most boring person on the planet."

"Not boring in any way or on any planet. You're a mix of sweet and sassy, and strength and vulnerability. Yet when it comes time for you to really put your foot down...you back off."

His words stung. She turned her head, peering at his profile, which was just as good to look at as the frontal view. "What about you? You present this I-don't-give-a-damn front.... Yet even when someone doesn't ask you for help, you're there." She narrowed her eyes. "Even when someone doesn't *want* help, you're there."

"You see, there's your stinger."

She opened her mouth to reply then closed it.

"No comeback?" he asked.

"No way am I going to talk about your stinger."

He laughed much harder and longer than her comment merited. A man thing. She filed that away in her mind.

When his laughter quieted, he brushed his thumb over her cheekbone. "I don't help everyone, sweetheart. Just you."

"Why?"

"Because you don't ask for it."

"You don't make sense."

"Life doesn't always make sense. Let's not talk." He rolled over and put his arms around the front of her shoulders. "Remember, I'm your teddy bear. Let me hold you and keep you warm."

"Why?"

He used his elbow to rise up and peer down at her. "Because sometimes it's just nice to know you aren't alone."

Tears filled her eyes. He started to bend down to kiss her and, without saying a word, she rolled over, her back to him.

He shifted to spoon his body against hers. And when she felt something pressing against an inappropriate body part—because he was a man, and she supposed they couldn't stop some things—she thought of telling him that teddy bears were supposed to be *soft*. Instead, she closed her eyes and said a small thank you for this. It was, after all, Thanksgiving Day.

***

She fell asleep within moments, her body loosened, her breaths even in sleep. He could tell her mouth was open, but she wasn't snoring.

If she did snore, he had the feeling he'd think it was cute.

After about twenty minutes, he slid his arm out from under her and rolled off the bed. She made a wordless sound of protest. He touched her shoulder and whispered, "Shhhh." She settled down with a long sigh. Her trust touched something inside his chest, and he had the odd thought that rust was chipping off his heart, one flake at a time.

Quickly, he stripped off his jeans and sweater then pulled the cover folded on the bottom of the bed over her. He turned off the light and got back in bed next to her, carefully, making the minimum amount of movement, not wanting to disturb her.

Finally, he was spooning against her again, his hard-on that had softened getting stiff again.

He shifted closer to her. It was a sweet torture. As sweet as she was. Nothing like...

His breath stopped. Olivia. Nothing like Olivia.

He breathed again. Olivia, whom he hadn't thought about all day.

Still holding Maddie, he closed his eyes and pictured his dark queen, in all her glamorous beauty. She was probably on a set in Canada today. Laughing with her fellow cast members about the American Thanksgiving traditions. Mocking them. She might eat a little turkey, but there would be no pie for her size-two figure. At night, she would go to her soon-to-be husband wearing one of her many short, silky robes. Near the bed, she would untie the matching silken belt then shrug out of the robe, letting it fall to the floor for the maid to pick up in the morning.

And then she would climb into bed and allow her very wealthy and very besotted fiancé to worship her perfect body.

He closed his eyes tighter, the cloying darkness returning. Pushing his nose against the back of Maddie's hair, he breathed in deeply, smelling her hair, her skin, forcing himself to think of Maddie not Olivia, to remember the stories she'd told him, the people she'd helped, her tenderness with her son and her cat.

His tension eased. Slowly he drifted into sleep, thoughts of Maddie keeping away the gloom.

***

Dog had been banished overnight to the barn where the heat from the cows kept him and his water from freezing. The woman had said, in a hard voice, that she didn't want him in the house tonight. "Guests" were coming. Dog wasn't sure what "guests" were, but wonderful smells escaped out of the house and traveled on the cold air into the barn to him, drifting through the scents of the cows and their wastes.

He stuck his nose out of a crack between two pieces of wood to smell the food better, even though he couldn't eat any of it. The woman would never let him. And if the

girl gave him food, her mother would yell at her, so it was better if she didn't.

But as he sniffed, he caught a whiff of something else. Him. His human.

The hurt filled him, so he wasn't hungry anymore, the hurt too raw and too big.

He needed the human, and the human needed him. There was a hole inside him, and once he and the human were together, the hole would fill up and go away.

Dog didn't know how he knew this, he just knew and didn't question. The human and he were supposed to be together, but something bad had happened, some disconnect, and they'd missed each other.

And now he was locked in this barn and couldn't get to him.

And more than that, the girl needed him badly. He had to stay with her.

He did the only thing he could do. Pulled his nose in, lifted his head, and howled out his heartbreak.

Other howls and barks returned to him on the cold air. Other dogs who were out in the cold. At least he was in the barn. But instead of comforting him, it just hurt more.

17

A *mreow* and a furry mouth rubbing against her jaw woke Maddie up. Her eyelids snapped open. Weak rays of sunlight seeped in through the window, and she knew just where she was and what the rod pushing against her left buttock was.

She jerked away from it and from him. Ginger jumped off the bed, and Maddie followed her, her moves much clumsier. When she peered over her shoulder, she saw Logan had turned onto his back and was gazing up at her. His mouth was set, and she couldn't tell what he was thinking. Not with his brain, at least.

"Do you always wake up like that?" she asked.

"So handsome?" His right eyebrow rose, and he crossed his hands beneath the back of his head.

"So ready." She let her gaze travel down his body. He had a cover over him—a good idea since it was literally freezing out, and the insulation in the old house wasn't the best. But she let her eyes linger on the elevation below his waist. "Do you always wake up like that?"

"Always. And good morning to you, too."

She turned away from him. Some things it was better not to discuss with a man.

Ginger was already padding away, and she hurried downstairs after her. Zach should still be sleeping, and if she—

"Mom!" Zach looked up at her from the bottom of the stairway. "Are you upstairs with Logan? I woke up and couldn't find you."

"Um, I went upstairs to find Ginger."

He frowned, and she froze. Then he nodded. "Can we go to the hill today and ski?"

"Uh, sure." She worried about him on the ski hill, but she wouldn't let her fear hold him back. She made sure he wore a helmet and stayed with the younger kids, then tried to act like she wasn't a crazy, helicopter mom.

Today would be worse than usual. By now, she suspected the board members were leaking their version to their relatives, neighbors, and friends. Putting themselves in a good light and showing her as jealous and bitter.

The thought made her feel sick. Partially because there was some truth in it. She'd convinced herself that they liked her and wouldn't betray her. That her ex and her mother weren't the norm, they were the exceptions.

Now she was learning that the exceptions were her sister and Caroline...and one more. Logan. The man she'd thought would be least likely to stand by her.

She smiled determinedly at Zach. She wasn't going to hide away from any gossip as if she were at fault. Instead, she was going to march in with her head held high. "Let me shower and change then I'll get you breakfast, okay, sweetie?"

"Can I watch TV?"

She nodded. Whatever happened, Zach came first. In the end, he was the one that mattered. Not her hurt feelings, not her dented ego. Whatever she decided to do about the situation would come down to deciding what was best for Zach.

***

Logan looked down at the three words on his phone: *I need you.*

His heart pounding fast and his hands numb, he headed to the window, the cell phone in his hand, and stared out at the bare branches of the treetops. Someone must have taught Olivia how to text. Maybe her fiancé.

The phone trilled, and he looked down at it again. *Call me. I need you.*

I needed you, he thought. And where were you?

But he knew the answer to that question.

With another man.

On an impulse, he unlocked the window and pushed it up, slowly, because it wanted to stick. Then there was a storm window to open, too. He started on it, the need to throw out the damn phone compelling him on. But as he tugged on the damn metal tabs at the bottom of the old windows, he remembered he couldn't do it.

This was the number he'd given the investigator he'd hired to find out the dirt on Duane.

He needed the phone for Maddie.

And how dramatic was he to need to throw the phone out the window into the snow? Like a damn diva.

He'd accused Maddie of being afraid of rejection, but look how he was acting.

His jaws clamped, he turned off the phone then set it on the dresser. He even remembered to close the window before heading downstairs for breakfast.

He was getting so domesticated it wasn't funny.

He ran down the stairs. In a short time, he'd be out of

here. He'd stay through Christmas, and then he'd leave and put the house up for sale.

Or maybe he'd let Maddie stay here. It would mean nothing to him. He didn't belong here, and she did.

And if she was pregnant...

He reached the bottom and put that thought out of his mind. If she was, he would deal with it then.

18

During the next week, Maddie felt as if she had a target on her back. Instead of dying down during the second week, the fallout got worse. While shopping during her lunch hour on the second Friday, she heard whispers, felt pointed stares, and saw lopsided pity smiles. In the grocery store coffee aisle, Ruth Johnson patted her on the head as if she were a hurt puppy. In the cereal aisle, she hurried away from Arnie Johnson, who was lifting his hand to pat her, too. And she was pretty sure Arnie's landing target wasn't her head.

Like the Bonnie Raitt song said, people were talking— and she suspected some of them were tweeting and Facebooking, too.

To assuage her nerves, she picked up a bag of dark chocolate truffles. Back in the town hall office, she gave Caroline her requested package of ginger tea. Caroline thanked her profusely, telling her how the tea helped her digestion—a subject Maddie tried to avoid. When Maddie took out the bag of truffles, Caroline's eyebrows shot up.

"What happened? Someone said something, right?"

"The news is out," Maddie said.

"I didn't say anything. I bet it was Helen."

"My money's on George." Maddie unwrapped a truffle. "He'll want to twist it to put himself in the most sympathetic light. And he and Duane have tons of relatives who live around here."

"Sure, they do, but how many of them like George and

Duane?"

"You know them better than I do."

"George and Duane aren't favorites around here." Caroline rubbed the pads of her thumb and middle finger together to show there was money involved. "The only kindnesses they do are for themselves. Not like you. You've got more friends in this town than they do."

"Blood is still thicker."

"If you're a vampire."

Maddie laughed, but she heard the bitter notes in it. If her laughter was chocolate, she'd spit it out.

"Hey, it's not all bad." Caroline headed to the hot water carafe to pour herself a cup to dip her tea bag into. "What about all the dates you've lined up?"

Taking the chair on the other side of Caroline's desk, Maddie slumped into it. Since her work was cut in half, she'd had a lot of time to spend online this week, looking at cat pictures and checking for matches.

It was more fun looking at cat pictures. They were cuter than the men, and she was pretty sure they weren't Photoshopped.

"I haven't accepted any yet."

"You should. The inventor sounds interesting. Eighty-nine patents! You never know, one of them might come through, and you could be married to a billionaire."

"That wasn't on my list of must-haves."

"Put it on. If you can't use the money, you can send some my way. I always dreamed of a trip to Paris." She sighed and gazed out of the window. After her husband had died, she'd used his life insurance policy and the money she got from selling their house on Angel Lake to put her two children through college.

"If I marry a billionaire," Maddie said, "even a millionaire, I'll send you to Paris. First class all the way."

Caroline crossed back to Maddie's desk, her cheeks pushed up in a giant smile. "And I'll take that trip."

They both laughed, and the light seemed brighter in the office than a moment ago.

"If you didn't like the sound of the inventor," Caroline said, sitting in her chair, "what about the IT guy from Minnesota? Just think, if you have a problem with your computer, he could fix it."

"Hard to pass up a guy like that."

"I know. And he's a dad, too. Divorced."

"That's what they all say."

Caroline opened her eyes wide in mock surprise. "You mean they might be lying?" She grinned. "My favorite is the trumpet player in Madison. At least you know he looks like his picture. He was really cute on that YouTube video. And when he's not playing for the orchestra, he likes jazz. You know that's my favorite music."

"Why don't I juggle all three of them? The inventor in case he gets rich, so I can send you to Paris. The IT guy to take care of your computer. And the trumpet player so you can drool over his looks and his music."

"Sounds like a great plan to me."

"I think you were a cat in another life," Maddie said. "Somehow God put you into a woman's body by mistake."

"I've often thought the same thing. Who wouldn't rather be a cat than a woman? Just think, you let people worship you, pet you, and take care of you, and if you

don't like what they do, you scratch and bite them."
Caroline leaned forward. "Why make the three men wait?
Is it because of Logan?"

"Not the way you think." She frowned at her
chocolate. She doubted Caroline would guess she was
careless enough to have had unprotected sex and might
be pregnant.

What the hell had she been thinking?

Oh, right, she hadn't been thinking.

"I have to tell Logan a story every night, remember?"
she said. "I have to be home for that."

"You can record your stories for him. He doesn't need
you in the same room. I'm sure if you ask, he'll give you a
night off. He doesn't seem like a demanding Hollywood
guy at all." Her voice ended with a high note of surprise.

"Doesn't matter. My life is in flux right now, and it's
probably not a good time to date." That was the truth in
too many ways. "Instead of looking for a date, I should
spend all my time looking for a job."

"This is a bad time to look for employment, just
before Christmas. Did you hear back about the job in
Ohio?"

Maddie shook her head. When she hadn't been
looking for men, she'd been emailing resumes. She hated
to be too far from her sister's family, but she might not
have a choice.

"Damn these board members." Caroline's face
tightened into an angry cat fierceness. "They've been on
it so long, they think they can do anything they please.
It's been the same members for twelve years now, and
Patty and Victor have been on it for twenty years."

"I've only been here for five years." Maddie tried to smile, but her mouth wouldn't cooperate. "No wonder they feel they don't owe me anything. To them, I'm a newcomer."

"You sure you're not going to sue? You have grounds."

"Don't tell them, because I hope they're squirming, but I'm pretty sure I won't."

Caroline put her elbow on the desktop and tapped her thin upper lip with her index finger. "I might see what I can do."

Maddie leaned over the desk and hugged her, unshed tears clogging her throat. Then she picked up her bag of truffles and headed to her own office. She actually had work to do before the day's end. And besides, all she could think of was the pregnancy test she was going to take tomorrow morning.

***

Logan had never thought his life might be changed by the results of a pee test. But here he was, up a good hour earlier than usual, hovering in the downstairs hallway with Zach, who gazed up at him, his head tilted.

"Is the upstairs toilet broke?" Zach asked.

Logan heard a flush from inside the bathroom. He'd read the instructions on the box, which said she had to wait a few minutes to see the results. He wasn't sure why he was anxious. He didn't know why he hadn't used a condom, either. First time that had ever happened. Even with Olivia, he'd never once forgotten.

But with Olivia, sex had been a game. They'd both

used it to see who would win.

With Maddie, it was...something else. Tenderness and passion. He hadn't been thinking with his brains. His body had been in control.

But that was a lie. Something else had been in control.

His emotions.

He frowned. Now he understood why this bothered him. Emotions were impractical. Not like his addiction to Olivia. He understood that. His addiction had come out of the force of her power and her beauty, the danger that she might drop him any second for someone new.... The combination created an adrenaline rush he couldn't resist.

But he couldn't think of that now. Not with the small boy waiting for his answer.

"It's working," he said finally. "But I'm in no rush."

"Sometimes Mom takes a long time."

"She's a woman. That's what they do."

"Because they don't have a penis?"

A noise coming from the bathroom sounded suspiciously like a growl.

"Could be. They have to pull down their pants, and that's an extra step."

Zach nodded, and another sound came, this one a clear "argh."

Logan bent to the same height as the four-year-old. "I think your mom doesn't like us talking about this."

Zach laughed, the sound clear and pure, like a church bell ringing. As Logan watched Zach's laughing face, something inside him opened up, and he thought he would like a child. Especially if Maddie was the child's mother. She was good at it, the way she was good at telling stories and making him forget he was supposed to be miserable.

The toilet flushed again, a sound of finality. He snapped up, his muscles tense again, and Zach frowned, obviously feeling his nerves.

Water rushed from the faucet next.

He leaned against the wall. Next to him, Zach copied his stance. Logan glanced down at him. If Zach had chosen him as a role model, he'd picked the wrong man. He was a selfish man and wouldn't be around long enough to help nurture him or any child.

At least he could support his child. She wouldn't have to worry about money. He was thirty-three, with no ties, and—

The door opened; she stepped out. He pushed away from the wall, not saying anything. She shook her head. A no.

A smile that looked painful formed on her face, and she bent down and picked up Zach, twirling him in the small hallway. Zach's laughter rang out, and Logan stepped sideways, steering clear of Zach's feet.

She slowed to a stop, still holding her laughing son, her back to Logan. She glanced over her shoulder at him. "I'm making oatmeal. Steel cut. I soaked it overnight, so it won't take long to make. Do you want some?"

He nodded, not opening his mouth, unable to speak, not sure what would come out of his mouth if he tried. She set Zach down, and they headed to the kitchen, hand in hand, Zach telling her that Logan had been waiting a long time to use the bathroom.

As they turned into the kitchen, the numbness still hovered around Logan. Though the sun shone brightly, the day felt oppressive. Tinged with gray. Maybe something in the atmosphere. Maybe another storm was coming.

He stepped inside the bathroom, bent down, and picked up the test stick. The marking still showed on the stick, a minus symbol. He stared at it for a long moment before dropping it back in the trash, because he couldn't deny the rush of sorrow squeezing his heart.

***

Tires rolling on gravel woke Dog up from his nap in the barn. The girl's mother had banished Dog here again, because they were "expecting company," and she didn't want him to "stink up the place."

Dog was glad to get away from her sharp voice that cut into his ears like the edge of a flat stone, but he should be inside to guard the house. As the car neared, he smelled the people inside, a woman and a man—he could tell the differences in their scent—and there was a stronger scent.

Dog peeked through the space between two wall boards in time to see a tall man open the rear door and take out a cage. A small animal was inside the cage, white and fluffy. Dog couldn't tell by looking at it if it was a dog or cat, but he smelled dog. His nose was never wrong.

"Erin's going to be so happy," a woman said, and the door opened.

The woman went in first, the man with the cage following her.

The next second, Dog heard the girl squeal, then the woman laughed and said, "I knew you'd love Snowball. We bought her for you."

19

The scare was over, but the repercussions continued. It changed Logan.

It changed Maddie, too.

He became more polite, more distant, spending more time upstairs and less downstairs. Yet he still came down for his story every night. And every night, he smoldered like a brush fire about to burst into full flame, sending her to bed aching and wanting.

And now, days later, he showed up in the kitchen before she went to work, still smoldering.

He was killing her. Slowly.

Not really, of course...it just felt like he was driving her crazy by slow degrees. She was always so practical, but around him, her practicality was blown away. Far, far away.

"Where's Zach?" he asked.

"On the bus going to school, like he does every morning." She put a slice of pumpkin bread into a baggie for her morning snack.

"Can you meet me at lunch today?"

She dropped the baggie into her purse and hoped the pumpkin bread didn't get crushed. "I could, but why should I?" As she said it, she realized how hostile she sounded. She frowned. She didn't mean it that way. She just meant... Oh, she didn't even know what she meant.

The slow crazy was speeding up.

"It would be to your advantage," he said.

She looked at the wall clock shaped like a cartoon duck. "When people say that, the advantage usually heads straight to them."

"You're turning into a cynic."

"Maybe I've caught that from you." As soon as she said the words, she clamped her teeth shut. Now she sounded bitter, and that's not what she wanted to be.

"Perhaps you have," he said, not showing any emotion. "Are you coming to lunch with me or not? Your choice."

She sucked in a breath then exhaled shakily. "Sure, I'll be there."

He gave her the name of a restaurant she was familiar with in Eagleton. Nodding, she put on her shoes then headed to her car where she realized she'd put on her other pair of slippers instead of her shoes and had to go back for them.

He was in the exact place she'd left him two minutes ago.

His phone was ringing, the sound coming from upstairs. The notes from "Witchy Woman."

She paused, but the darkness in his eyes had her backing away, though he kept his lips together, not saying anything.

Until she reached the door.

"Do you know that if you don't want to receive calls from a certain number, you can block it?" she asked.

Without waiting for an answer, she wrenched open the door. And thank God, the door didn't stick, and she was out of there before he could say anything. She had the feeling when she was at lunch with him, she wouldn't have much of an appetite.

***

Dog was free, but as he ran, his leg hurt, the one he'd injured. It was better now than before he found the man in the barn, but it had never healed right. Despite the pain, he kept on running.

The girl would cry, he knew it, but she had the new puppy. A little fluffy thing the mother liked to put on her lap. She said it was a ball of trouble, but it reminded her of a dog she had when she was little.

The dog made both of them happier. When they were happier, the man was happier, too.

And then the woman would look at Dog, and her face would tighten. Dog could feel her temper building, could smell the bitter edge in the scent coming off her skin. He knew about angry people.

And he knew about people who weren't angry, too. People who tried to help him.

But they weren't his human.

He needed his human, and all he had to do was follow the scent in the air to find him. A small wisp of a smell that was there for him alone.

He slowed, limping, on the road where there wasn't any snow. Every now and then, a few cars raced by him. One stopped, and a woman called to him, but he ran up on the snow. He wouldn't come down, not even when she held food out and called to him, "Eat! Eat! Eat!"

He knew what "eat" meant. That had been one of the first words he'd learned.

Finally, she set the food on the snow then got into her truck and drove away. Dog quickly ran to the food and gobbled it up. Then he ran again. He had a long way to go to reach his human. He'd been through three winters already, and this was the first time he'd smelled him. He feared if he didn't reach him soon, his human might go away, and he'd never smell him again.

***

Caroline had been giggling all morning, shooting Maddie looks that made her nervous as she said good-bye. The nervousness stayed with her as got into her car and drove to Eagleton. It was better to think about Caroline than Logan, especially since she was meeting Logan at the Audubon Restaurant in the Audubon Hotel. The old Victorian hotel was one of the loveliest places in town. The restaurant was the best in the area, but Maddie's mind kept switching from Caroline to the rooms in the hotel.

She'd heard that two people could easily fit into the bathtubs.

That they jetted out warm water.

That they were romantic in an old-world way, some of them with satin sheets and lace drapes. It was the go-to place for wedding nights, anniversaries, and one-night stands for the wealthy.

Logan was very wealthy.

But why not just ask her to meet him at home? *His* home, she reminded herself. Unless he was hoping to seduce her. After all, she'd said no more sex, and he seemed to agree.

She'd meant what she said.

But if he leaned over her and breathed on her neck...

She sighed.

If he lowered his voice and told her that he loved the small squeaking sounds she made when she orgasmed...

A breathy moan came out of her mouth.

If he even picked up her foot and insisted on giving her another foot rub...

She mewed like Ginger when she wanted to be petted.

Her hands tightened on the steering wheel. She had it bad. The hotel was in sight already, and she slowed. The fifteen-minute drive had flown by, and thoughts of Caroline had flown out of her head.

Telling herself it wasn't likely that he'd invited her to seduce her—a man as sophisticated as him had to know that it wasn't the locale that mattered—she marched into the restaurant. He was at the table already, turning to look at her, as if he'd sensed her.

Right. In her dreams.

She told the greeter that she saw her table then headed to it, realizing Logan wasn't alone. A man was seated across from Logan. Tall, bulky, and dark-skinned, he looked like a former athlete. He wore a suit that fit him well, and he appeared to be in his forties with a receding hairline, his black hair in a buzz cut. As she reached the table, both he and Logan stood.

"Maddie, this is Bert Wittaker." Logan said.

Bert's hand engulfed hers, and he reminded her of a big dog that looked dangerous but was really gentle. Most of the time. They greeted each other, and she took a seat and glanced at the manila envelope on the empty setting across from her.

"What's this about?" she asked, noting there was a cup of coffee waiting for her.

"It's about changing your life," Logan said.

She looked down at the menu in front of her then back at Logan. "So we're not eating lunch?"

His eyes gleamed with humor. "I always feed my victims first."

"Lovely. What's the most expensive dish?"

Bert laughed, but Logan just looked at her with the burn back in his eyes. Seducing her without saying a word. She picked up the menu and opened it. If he weren't so damn rich, she really might order the most expensive meal in the place. But it would mean nothing to him, so she may as well order what she liked best.

She ended up ordering the crab cake appetizers and tomato soup for her meal. The first because it was a long time since she'd had good crab cakes. The second was comfort food.

The waitress collected their menus, and as soon as she left, she turned to Logan. "Now do you want to tell me what's in the envelope?"

Bert looked at Logan, who nodded. "I'm an investigator." He lowered his voice so it wouldn't carry to the nearby tables. "Logan hired me to find out why a certain Duane Frickmann lost his previous position as a town administrator."

She switched her gaze from him to Logan. "Ammunition," Logan said. "The more you have, the better a chance of getting in the best shot."

"What if I don't want to take a shot at him?"

"Then you're a quitter, and I don't think you're that."
He held her gaze. "This is for Zach. I didn't think you'd
let your hurt feelings matter more than your son."

She stiffened. Damn him. He was right.

"What do you have?" She turned back to Bert. "Is it a
woman?"

"Nope, money." He handed her the manila folder. "He
and the town treasurer were in it together."

She grimaced then read the pages quickly. The
numbers were in the high six figures, and she had to stop
herself from exclaiming. Finally she looked up. "How
come he's not in jail?"

"He and the treasurer paid back every penny they
stole," Bert said, "plus interest, and the town agreed to
not prosecute them."

"They didn't want to embarrass themselves." Logan's
voice was as dry as her throat.

She took a zip of her tea as Bert said his informant
had told him the town board hadn't shared this
information with the town or the local sheriff. It was all
done through lawyers.

"Did the town give him a reference?" she asked.

"I doubt it." Bert said. "If he pulled the same trick
again, it's possible they'd be liable. He's lucky he's not in
jail."

"Then this information isn't available to anyone?" she
asked. "How did you get it?"

He grinned, his teeth white. "You don't know who I
am, do you?"

"A football player?"

"Never mind. Let's just say that I have a few rabid fans, and they're likely to tell me anything."

"It's the celebrity thing." Logan grimaced. "It melts brain cells. So what are you going to do with this?"

She kept her gaze on Bert. "You know I'm going to look you up when I get back to the office."

"I'm sure you will."

"Do you work nearby?"

"Minneapolis. One of the reasons Logan hired me for this."

"He has his own agency," Logan said.

"I could tell that by the way his suit fits him."

Bert shouted a laugh, either not noticing or not caring about the way people looked at him, their faces lighting up.

"I've been thinking lately that I could do something more interesting than being a town administrator." She gave him her you're-going-to-like-me smile. "Are there any positions open in your agency that I could fill?"

"My card is in the report." He gestured at the folder. "Send me your resume."

Logan tapped his fingernails on the table. Bert turned to him. "You got a problem?"

"No problem here." Logan narrowed his blue eyes at Maddie. "He's not going to pay you anywhere near what the town will pay you."

Before she could say anything, Bert leaned toward him, inches from Logan's face. "If you're trying to stop me from hiring her, you just made a big mistake. You know I always rise to a challenge." He turned back to Maddie. "Definitely send your resume. You're a smart woman, and I can tell you're honest. Two of the top qualities I look for in an employee. I'll find something for you, and I guarantee the pay will make you happy."

Her face warmed. "I'll do that. Thank you."

The rest of the meal went by quickly, and she talked and laughed, but it felt as if she were split in two. One part of her talking, and the other part marveling at her nerve and the possibilities ahead for her.

This must be similar to what Oscar winners said afterward, that they couldn't remember saying their speeches. As if speaking through a fog.

Then she was standing and telling the men she had to go back to work. Bert reminded her to take the folder with her. Logan said he'd bring it home for her, and Bert grinned, his eyebrows raised. Logan gave him a glance that should have singed Bert's eyebrows off, and the big man just grinned wider.

She grinned too, feeling as if this were all a game. And for once, she was on the winning side.

***

"What happened to the vampiress?" Bert asked.

Logan spit the coffee he'd just sipped back into the cup, and Bert roared with laughter. A big man with a big laugh and a big personality.

He was still sniggering when Logan said, "Last I heard, she was about to be married."

"No shit. I didn't think she'd ever remove her claws from you."

"You didn't like her?"

187

The humor in Bert's face blanked, his eyebrows contracting. "She's some kind of a throwback to Cleopatra. Or maybe the Sirens."

"The dark queen," Logan said.

"The evil Disney queens. I can see that. So she finally retracted her hooks and let you swim free." He gestured toward the empty chair. "I think you caught a good one there."

"She's not mine."

"Maybe not. But you want her."

"She's not that kind of woman."

"I don't know what you mean by that. If you want to pay me to check it out, I wouldn't complain."

"I bet you'd check it out."

Laughter sparked in Bert's eyes. "You want to slug me, don't you?"

"Nah. I don't want my fist broken. Besides, you'd be wasting your time. She wouldn't want you."

"Is that another challenge?"

He froze for a couple beats of his heart then shrugged, as if she meant nothing to him. "I'll pass. If I said yes, you're so competitive you'd probably go after her."

"Smart of you to back down." Bert winked at him. "I'd do more than just go after her. I'd win her, too."

Logan sat back, not saying anything, knowing deep inside, wherever that place of *knowing* was, that Maddie wouldn't give in to Bert, no matter what Bert did. She wanted just one man.

Him.

And he wanted her, but he was no good for her—and she was too good for him. He was writing now, and as soon as his screenplay was done, he would be gone like snow in summer.

20

Dog ran down a country road at a quick, steady pace. He liked the country better than cities. In cities, there were more cars and people and other dogs. Cities didn't have places for him to lie down. No places to hide while he rested. Twice today, he'd been chased by cars. In the city, he'd been chased by cars, bikes, and people on foot.

So far, he'd outrun and outsmarted them, even with his bad leg. But it hurt to run on it too long.

Some days he wondered if he'd ever reach his human. But he never stopped. Never. His human needed him, and he needed his human. Being without his human was a hole inside him.

And this morning, the sky was bright and, even though it was cold enough for Dog to see his breath, the sun warmed him. This morning, he could smell his human more sharply than the other mornings.

He was getting closer. Eagerness was building in him, like snow, with one snowflake landing on another until it was as high as his tail. He ran faster and faster and—

A horn blared. He jumped, and a car sped by him, so close he felt a rush of hot air, and then the bad smells from the back end of the car rushed into his face. Swerving to get away from the smell, he put too much weight on his sore leg. He tumbled to the road, stones sticking past his matted fur and into his legs. Pain tore through him, and he lay there, whimpering.

Then he stopped whimpering and got to his feet and ran again. Slower than before, limping more than before, but still going.

As long as Dog could smell his human, nothing was going to stop him.

***

The perfect Saturday morning was going to make it harder for Maddie to leave Angel Lake. The sun was bright, and the smell of chocolate chip cookies baking in the oven filled the house while they put up the tree. She even prevailed on Logan to go to the store to get ornament hooks so she could decorate the tree.

"They have them at the grocery store?" he asked.

"They have deodorant at grocery stores, don't they? Why not hooks?"

His expression looked pained, and she laughed at him. So did Zach, flopping off the chair and onto the living room carpet.

Logan left, and she wondered what his sophisticated friends would say if they saw him at the store buying ornament hooks. Then she decided they went to stores and bought things for themselves, too, and she started setting her decorations around the house. The Drummer Boy music box, the angel kicking a football, the nutcrackers, the Santas, the train...

She tended to go a little overboard for the holiday.

Logan had put the lights on the tree when she'd started the cookies. He'd told Zach it was a man's job, making Zach giggle. She'd looked up from her measuring cup filled with flour just as Zach stopped laughing and watched Logan with total concentration, as if he were memorizing his every move. The look on his face had put a lump in Maddie's throat.

The last batch was in the oven now, with more cookies cooling on the counter and others already in boxes. She knelt in front of a storage box that she'd labeled "GLASS." She directed Zach to the non-glass decorations. With Logan at the store, it was just the two of them.

She waited for a sense of relief, but it didn't come. Neither did a sense of sorrow, and she was glad for that. She didn't want to be like her mother, who was only happy when a man paid attention to her.

As she was hooking a glass reindeer ornament on the tree a moment later, she heard the door open and close then Zach's laughter and Ginger's meows...

And was that noise an ornament rolling on the floor?

She turned in time to spot Ginger rolling an ornament toward the hall while Zach laughed again.

"Zach!" She was on her feet as Logan's chuckles joined Zach's. "Don't let Ginger play with the ornaments."

"She likes it, Mom!"

"Maybe she likes it, but I don't."

"It's plastic, isn't it?" Logan set the bag on the kitchen table then took off his jacket. "Let them have fun."

She glared at him then took a deep breath before turning to Zach. Seeing the uncertainty in his face, she felt guilty, though she was saying the same thing that nearly every other mother on the planet would say to her son.

"Just this once," she said. "And next time ask me first."

He beamed at her before turning to Ginger, who'd stopped playing as if to listen to her, too. "We can play!" Zach said.

As if Ginger really did understand what he'd said, she whacked the round ornament down the hall toward the bedrooms. Laughing, Zach chased after her, with the cat dashing ahead of him, out of Maddie's sight.

"You have more than hooks in that bag." She nodded at the bag on the kitchen table.

"Nuts. And a nutcracker." He nodded at the decorative nutcrackers on the fireplace mantle. "Ones that really crack nuts."

"I'm so bad at using them."

"I'll crack them for you." He frowned then, and she frowned, too.

It felt as if they were a couple instead of two people sharing a house for a short time. Cohabiting and not comingling—except for that one incident, which hadn't been repeated. Nor had it been forgotten, at least not by her, about twenty times a day. She supposed he hardly gave it a thought.

The oven buzzed, and she headed to the kitchen. The cookies looked perfect. She set one pan on the pullout breadboard and the other on top of the stove.

Logan came to her side. "Guess what happened at the store?"

"You ran into Michelle Shiffly?"

"Who's that?"

She put the cooled cookies into the cookie jar. "Never mind."

"Someone else you let stay here? That's it, isn't it?"

"Just think of all the good deeds you did." She grabbed the spatula and turned to the first cookie sheet and shimmied cookies off it and onto the cooling rack. "If it wasn't Michelle, who was it?"

"I was asked to sign a petition to recall the board members."

Her head snapped up. "Holy shit. Caroline."

"Your co-worker? It said 'Citizens Who Care.'"

Maddie's throat clogged with emotions, and tears dampened her eyes. She swallowed before she could speak. "I don't know if she can be a public part of it, since she's an employee, but I bet she's behind it." She dropped the spatula and grabbed a napkin from the napkin holder to pat away tears. "She's crazy. I have to call her." She sniffed. "As soon as I finish this."

"I'll finish it." Logan picked up the spatula then grabbed the other pan of cookies.

"Mom?" Zach's tone was plaintive. "Are you okay?"

She turned and saw him staring up at her, his expression scared. She swooped down to hug him. "It's wonderful, honey, just wonderful."

"Those are happy tears," Logan said. "If you're going to be around women a long time, you'd better get used to it."

Zach switched his gaze to Logan, his eyes big, as Maddie groaned. "Men cry happy tears, too." She pointed at Logan, who was pushing the cookies off the spatula with his hands. "And before you touch the cookies, wash your hands."

Before he could say anything, she grabbed her phone from the counter, Zach giggling behind her.

A minute later, she had Caroline on the phone. "I know what you did," she said.

Caroline cracked up. "We already have over four hundred signatures. We only need twenty-five hundred to get a new election."

"Idiot. You can get fired for this."

"Ha! As long as I do my work, they can't get rid of me. Let them try to fire me. I dare them. Or maybe we should both walk. If that happens, they'll be in big trouble."

Maddie sat heavily in the chair at the kitchen table as Zack ran to play with Ginger in the hallway. "I love you, Caroline, but don't lose your job over me."

"They won't dare. I have too many relatives who vote. And they all have big mouths, too."

"Who else is doing this with you? Alma, right?"

"Of course. And Dexter. They're your fans."

"I love them, too."

"And everyone you helped, and their families."

"That wasn't me. That was Logan." She glanced at him, and one side of his mouth was jerked up and so was one eyebrow.

She turned her head away.

"Maybe the house was his, and he gave you permission," Caroline said, "but everyone knows you're the one who championed them. There's no way he would've known unless you told him. And guess what this means?"

"I'm awful at guessing." And she didn't need any

more surprises today. She was wrung out by them.

"It means you can't leave. We're all fighting for you, and you have to fight for you, too."

She winced. "Caroline, you're evil."

Caroline gave a witch's cackle then said she had to go to hand out more petitions. She hung up before Maddie could say anything.

Setting down the phone, Maddie saw Logan leaning against the counter, not even pretending he hadn't been listening.

"I suppose you're going to say something," she said and heard the huskiness of her voice. This had been so...unexpected. Maybe more unexpected than the stab in her back by the board members.

"You'll save them a lot of effort and printing costs if you tell the board you know why Duane was fired."

"Blackmail them," she said, hearing the flatness in her voice.

"Some people deserve to be blackmailed." He stepped toward her. From Zach's room, she could hear him playing chase-the-cat, a game he never won. Ginger was not only twenty times faster than him, when she got tired of playing, she hid in places where no human could find her.

"Why don't you fight for your place?" Logan asked. "People are fighting for you, but you aren't fighting for yourself."

She looked down and then at the tree in front of the big living room window. Christmas was less than two weeks away, but she liked to buy a real tree, and some of them dried out so fast. When Christmas was over and the

New Year came, that's when she wanted to hold on to Christmas for as long as she could. And not Christmas, not really, but the love and the joy and the goodwill.

"I'm doing what I feel is right." She raised her chin and stared into his eyes.

He looked back for a long moment, as if he were trying to see all the way into her mind.

Good luck with that, she thought. Sometimes she didn't know why she did things.

And who was he to criticize what she did? Besides living in his house, of course. "What about you and your dark queen?" she asked.

He pulled back, and she stepped toward him, her arms out, cringing inside, wanting to take the words back. "I didn't—"

"Forget it. You're right. I'm not one to talk. What you do is none of my business." He turned toward the stairway.

"No, Logan, I'm..." She stopped. He reached the stairway and ran up the stairs as she closed her mouth and clenched her hands to keep herself from calling him back to her.

A meow and Zach's laugh pulled her attention to the hall where he was carrying Ginger toward her, his face lit up.

She forced herself to put on a smile, even as she wondered why she was messing up her life so badly. For the past five years, it had been going so smoothly.

And then *he* had come, forcing her to see that so much of the life she was leading really wasn't her own.

Now almost every part of her life was falling apart.

She bent down on her knees and hugged Zach and Ginger. Every part but this one, which was the part that mattered most.

"I love you."

"I love you, too, Mama."

The cat wiggled between them, and Maddie drew back so Ginger could jump loose, then she grabbed Zach again, hugging him for a long moment before he squirmed away, having enough hug time, and she let him go.

Sometimes it felt to her as if the only ones she trusted with her heart were her son and her cat. She was holding back from life, and that wasn't a good way to go.

She made up her mind. Tonight after Zach went to bed, she would tell Logan he was right about her. And tell him why.

Her throat tightened, and she had to consciously breathe.

Just thinking about it scared her. But maybe, once she told him, she wouldn't have a reason to be afraid anymore.

21

By the time Logan headed downstairs for his story, the tree was up and so was Zach, who'd stayed up later tonight to help Maddie decorate. The living room looked warm and welcoming. Logan was used to professionally decorated homes for Christmas, meant to impress and wow instead of to brighten a heart. His parents had never been into decorating for the holidays. They'd had a small imitation tree that they put on the side table every year as they grumbled over moving their piles of books to make room for it.

Maddie was their opposite. The house had a mix of many holiday items, including a stuffed Santa with a bell inside it that rang every time Zach threw it at Logan and when he threw it back at Zach. Both of them laughing each time until Maddie told Zach it was time for him to go to bed.

As she made sure he brushed his teeth then tucked him in bed and kissed him good night, Logan threw the Santa up in the air and caught it, over and over. Ever since he'd made love to Maddie, his writing had come faster and easier. As if she were the antidote to whatever it was that had stopped him. Today, he'd written his next to last scene in the book.

Tomorrow he was going to write the unhappy ending.

The heroine wasn't going to die, but she was going to be alone, this woman who lived in a fairy-tale bubble and was afraid to come out of her room. She was a prisoner of her insecurity.

He'd wanted an unhappy ending, and he'd gotten it. It should make him happy.

"You want something to drink?" she asked.

He dropped the Santa on the floor. "Sure. Whatever you have."

"Spiced wine?"

Turning, he saw her heading to the kitchen in her tan slippers, Green Bay Packers sweatpants and a sweatshirt with a Christmas tree design.

"Anything but that," he said.

She laughed shortly. When she came back, she handed him a brandy. She had a glass of red wine for herself that she sipped before sitting on the couch, her legs stretched out on the ottoman.

"About what you said earlier—"

"Forget it." He held out one hand, as if to stop her words. "I don't want to hear about it."

She looked down, and her shoulders hunched. He could practically see her crawling back into her shell. She seemed so brave, but her bravery roared out for other people. Her son, mostly, but also the people she helped. Even the cat, who was the reason she'd ended up here.

When it came to herself, her bravery shrank.

"Once upon a time," she said, her voice falling and rising into her storytelling rhythm, "there was a miller's daughter."

"There's always a miller's daughter," he said.

"They were very common at the time. Must have been something in the bread, because millers and their wives seemed to propagate easily. And not all millers' wives were happy about having so many children. They wished their husbands would stick their equipment in another mill, if you know what I mean."

"I can follow the dots." He sat back, sipped his brandy, and wondered where this story would take her.

"This miller's wife was different. She only had two daughters, and the older one left, which left her with just one at home. But even one was too much for the mother. To put it plainly, her mother was not happy spending money on her daughter. She would rather spend her time and money on herself and her new husband."

"New husband? Not the miller?"

"No, the miller had to go to a faraway land to protect the king. While he was gone, his wife found another man."

"So she's not really the miller's wife anymore."

"No. But their daughters are still the miller's daughters. And now that the mother was stuck home with her daughter, she became mean."

"Why?"

"Because that's her nature. And you can't change your nature."

"Sure, you can. Laughter, a few friends, a few drinks—"

"The miller's ex-wife did a lot of drinking, but it didn't make her happy. It just made her meaner."

"She was a bitch." He set down his glass.

"In fairy tales, they're called witches."

"Are you sure it's a fairy tale?"

She frowned at him. "Witch or bitch, her mother wasn't nice to her. No matter what she did, good or wonderful, her mother didn't love her. The girl used to envy Cinderella, not for the prince, but because Cinderella's real mother had loved her."

He stared at her. Except for the furnace, and their voices, it was silent in the house. Cozy. With the lights on the Christmas tree, it felt...more intimate. Almost magical. "Cinderella's mother died. How could the girl be jealous?"

"Because she wanted her mother's love, and she never got it."

"And then what happened? It didn't end there, did it?"

"How do you think it ended?"

"I hope Prince Charming isn't coming to her rescue."

"Please. Prince Charming only did the easy stuff. Like kissing the sleeping princess. Dancing with her at a ball."

"That's true. I never heard of a prince kicking ass. My guess is the girl ended up with a boyfriend who used her and ended up beating her."

"Using her sounds about right. No beating her. That didn't happen."

"She was used to being undervalued. Not appreciated."

Instead of replying, she took a sip of her wine. It was hard to tell with the different colored lights on the tree reflecting on their faces, but he thought he saw the shimmer of tears in her eyes.

"She never fought for herself," he said, "or stood up for herself, because she tried that when she was a kid and always got shot down."

"Or punished." Her voice cracked.

"She was a piece of work, the miller's wife. But the daughter can change."

"She knows that now. It's on her radar. In fact, the daughter recently found some evidence that would help her get rid of her nasty boyfriend. But she..." She took another sip. "But she..." She sighed and took another sip.

"Was advised that she should use it," he said, taking over the storytelling.

"Well, yes."

"And instead of thanking her advisor, she turned on him."

She narrowed her eyes at him. "I wouldn't put it like that."

"I would. In fact, it's my guess he was surprised at her sudden timidity—"

"Timidity?" She sat straight, radiating indignity.

"Yes. She was usually someone who seemed pluckier."

"Plucky? Perhaps you should wait for the storyteller to tell the story. The storyteller doesn't care for the word *plucky*. It sounds like a feather pulled out of a turkey's butt."

"You have a way with words."

Her close-mouthed smile held as much humor as a prune. "Thank you. Now—" Her phone rang. She looked toward the kitchen. The phone rang again. She stood. "It might be important. My life is a little crazy now. I'd better answer it." As she walked away, she glanced behind her. "That's what a *plucky* heroine would do."

He watched her leave, half smiling. Now he understood, though she hadn't told him the real story. Just a few sentences. But with a good storyteller, a few sentences painted a big picture.

In less than a minute, she hurried back to him, holding her cell phone out. "For you. Someone says he's your friend. Cyril."

He stiffened. The only Cyril he knew was Olivia's personal trainer. Maddie stopped in front of him. "He says it's important."

As if the phone were a snake, he reached for it carefully. As soon as he took it, Maddie snapped around and crossed back to the kitchen.

"What is it?" Logan asked.

"Is that a good way to greet an old friend?"

"An old friend would call me on my phone."

"Perhaps if you'd reply to old friends who called you, your old friends wouldn't have to go through irregular channels."

He scowled at the phone. He'd only given Maddie's phone number to his personal assistant. "Don't call this phone number again."

"Oooh, you sound like you mean it. I've got shivers."

Logan looked at the Santa Claus clock on the mantel. One minute. He'd give Cyril one minute, and if he didn't give him the answer by then, he'd—

"Ah, shit," Cyril said, "I may as well get this over with. She's dying." Cyril's voice roughened. "Olivia is dying."

Sound stopped. So did his breath. The air roared in his head instead of his lungs. Gasping, he closed his eyes to fight a cloying dizziness and a hard kick in his belly.

"What?" The word came out in a harsh whisper.

"She's in her home, with twenty-four-hour care. She wants to see you."

He set his lips together.

"You're coming, aren't you? Right after her prognosis, she got rid of Neil. You know she didn't really love him. You're the real love of her life."

He sat like a lump, still not saying anything. Processing all of this. Wondering if he could trust her even in this. Olivia would do anything to get her way.

"She's growing thinner by the day," Cyril said. "She looks like she did in the post-apocalyptic film."

Logan remembered. She'd lost weight carefully under the guise of Cyril and a dietitian, eating green smoothies until the sight of them made him want to throw them down the toilet. She'd been so thin it had frightened him. Her reviews had been stunning, but the movie had tanked at the box office. She'd been furious, though she'd hidden it in public. And he'd felt her fear that she was losing her clout.

That's when she'd begun dating the hotel magnate, getting her name in all the tabloids and entertainment shows once again. Because in Hollywood, it wasn't always *what* you did, it mattered just as much *who* you did.

"She told me you're her real love," Cyril said. "She wants to see you before she dies. Logan, you know what a proud woman she is. Yet she told me you wouldn't answer her phone calls or even read her texts. She *begged* me to call you. Just come and see her. That's not too much to ask, is it?"

Yes, he thought. Yes.

But if he said no, after she died, he might have regrets.

His mouth dry, he downed a gulp of brandy before replying. "How long does she have?"

"Her doctors won't give her a date. They only say it's incurable."

"I'll be there." He hung up then stood. "I have to go."

Heading back from the kitchen with a bowl of pistachios, Maddie frowned. "Go? Go where?"

"California. A friend is ill." Without waiting for her response, he headed for the stairs.

"I'm sorry," she said, but he was already thinking about travel time and even considering chartering a plane.

Olivia was dying. The thought numbed his mind and his heart. Feeling would come later. Right now he needed to get to her.

***

She waited for him to come down, sitting straight on the couch, her chin up, her muscles tense. She knew the second he saw her. The tortured look on his face closed up, leaving him expressionless, not giving anything away. As if his heart was contracting, she thought, making itself smaller to protect him from further hurt.

"You're leaving," she said. "For good."

"It's an emergency."

She got to her feet slowly, feeling old, her bones aching, her breaths short. "I don't think so. You won't be back."

He opened his mouth, but she stepped sideways, away from him. Right now she wished she were a long way away from him. She couldn't wait until he left the house and flew away to be with his witchy lover.

"I'll stay until after Christmas," she said, "and then I'm leaving. I'll be gone by the end of the year. I appreciate it that you didn't have me arrested, and I wish you and your friend well."

"She's dying, Maddie." He looked at her with bruised eyes. "Olivia is dying."

"I'm sorry for that. Good-bye." She strode away from him, to her bedroom. Inside her room, she closed the door but stood near it. For a moment, she didn't hear anything from the hallway. No footsteps.

Hope rose inside her. Maybe—

The footsteps sounded on the wooden floor, heading away from her. The wheels carrying the suitcase creaking. Seconds later, the outer door opened then closed.

Biting her lip to keep from crying out, she started to shake. Her legs didn't hold her up, and she slumped against the door. Still, she didn't cry. Instead, she listened for him to return. For him to tell her he'd come to his senses. That he'd been about to make a huge mistake.

Except there was no mistake. There was no relationship. They'd only had sex once, and they'd agreed they wouldn't do it again. Maybe it just felt like a relationship because every night she told him a story. Because she cooked for him and, while she was at work, he'd thrown her and Zach's clothes into the washer and dryer when he washed and dried his own. Because he'd gone to her sister's for Thanksgiving, and Kris and Cody liked him. Because he listened to her work woes, and he empathized and had even hired an investigator. Because he treated Zach and Ginger with kindness. Because he listened to her tell a story every night.

Maybe that's why she remained slumped against the door...and hoped.

But the seconds passed, and because she was listening so hard, she heard a car engine start up.

She closed her eyes, and her head hung down as she listened to the car drive away from the front of her house. Only when she couldn't hear it any more did she push away from the door. A meow came from the floor near her feet. She glanced down. Ginger looked up at her, mewling, her voice plaintive. Maddie sat on the edge of the bed, no tears falling from her burning eyes, and held Ginger, her heart numb.

It was over. He was gone and wasn't coming back.

She'd always known it was coming. She just hadn't known it would hurt quite this much.

22

Olivia was as frail as she was beautiful. She lay on the chaise in her sunroom. In contrast to the oranges and purples in the room that oddly came together to look beautiful, her face was the color of heavy cream before whipping, her eyes dark and mysterious as ever. Smiling wanly, she held up emaciated arms to him.

"Logan, you came. I missed you so much." Her whispery voice was thick with suffering and regrets.

He took her hands in his and perched on the edge of her chaise. "Of course I came."

"Because you pitied me." Her smile was heartbreakingly sad...yet his heart felt numb, not even a twitch.

"Never mind why. You're here. It's all I wanted. You're here." Her golden-brown eyes glowed. "I don't deserve your friendship or your love. Not after what I did to you. The minute you walked out, I was sorry."

He didn't answer. Instead, he thought of last night. How he'd walked out. And another woman had said when he came back, she would be gone.

"It's not the first time you played with my heart," he said.

"Yes, but this time it felt...final."

Last night had felt final, too.

He didn't expect Maddie to change her mind. After all, they'd never made any exchanges of affection, beyond that one night. And that had been sex, nothing more.

It had been hard to stay away from her after that as she told him a story every night, with humor and pathos, though he invariably missed a portion, which he needed her to repeat, as he imagined making love to her again and again, while her voice, with all its magic, wrapped around him.

Every night he wanted her. Every day. But she had a son, and they lived in his house.

There were some things he didn't do.

"What's wrong?" The sharpness in Olivia's voice made him glance down at her. Botox kept vertical frown lines from forming between her eyebrows, but her forehead moved. As an actress, she needed movement to express emotion.

"What does your doctor say?" he asked.

"I don't want to talk about it." Her voice lowered to a whisper again, and he could see by the way she sagged against the chaise that the burst of energy had taken away some of her vitality. "I'm alive now, and you're here. That's what I want to focus on. I can't tell you how happy that makes me."

As he squeezed her hands, her eyes sparked with vitality. Fully alive.

A suspicion awoke in him. A crazy thought, because she wouldn't go this far. She wouldn't do this to him.

"You still love me," she said, and she clasped his hands, her grip strong for a dying woman. "I knew it."

He jerked away from her grasp and stood. "You're playing me." The harshness of his voice didn't fit the room, didn't fit her filmy clothes, her faded color, or her thin frame. As jarring and out of place as a giant in a room full of midgets.

But he didn't give a damn, his brain firing, telling him she had always been slender. In her profession, to remain an A-list star, thinness was necessary. It would only take a week or two of drinking green shakes for her to appear emaciated. As for her complexion, her next role was as a World War II factory worker, and she had to be pale for that.

"Logan..." She tried to rise up and fell back, as if it were too hard for her. Her eyebrows fought to connect and failed. "How can you say that?" Anguish made her voice low and hushed. Anguish and good acting. "How can you think that of me?"

He looked around the room. "You're filming this aren't you?"

"Of course not." Her tone sharpened. "I'm sick. I'm dying. How could you say something like that? Do you think I'd trick you like that? Am I so awful that you'd mistrust me like that?"

He knew the tricks. A microphone could be anywhere, and he spotted a mirror that he suspected could contain a camera. And then a lamp and a flower arrangement about five feet from the chaise, too far from Olivia's chaise to be useful to her, but perfect for filming.

"Logan! Answer me."

"Here's my answer." He strode to the table, picked up the vase and dumped the contents out.

"Are you crazy?" she screamed as a microphone transmitter fell out.

He reached out to the lamp but pulled back his hand. If he pushed it over, someone would have to clean it.

That someone wouldn't be Olivia. Besides, he'd seen the transmitters. He didn't need any other proof.

His anger drained away, and he turned to look at Olivia. "I *was* crazy. Crazy for ten years. But not anymore. Good-bye, Olivia."

He strode toward the door as she screamed his name. He kept walking, and the next second, a body slammed onto his back. Olivia. Her arms wrapped around his shoulders, pressing against the front of his neck, her legs tight around his waist.

"You love me," she said, her voice ringing. "You have to love me."

He faltered then stepped forward again. Her arms tightened even more, but he kept going, reaching the mirror that he suspected had a camera on it. In the moment of silence as she caught her breath, he heard an audible click of a camera. She grabbed his hair and pulled before he could take another step.

"Stop this! You love me. You can't leave me."

She was like a wild animal on his back. He reached up and grabbed her left wrist, holding on tightly so she couldn't hurt him.

With a wild cry, she lifted her other hand, and her fingers went for his eyes. Instinct and quick reflexes made him catch that wrist, too. Her weight unbalanced him, though, and he tumbled sideways as the door to the hall flew open and two men in jeans flew in, her publicist and favorite cameraman who Logan suspected was banging Olivia.

They were shouting something, and then the cameraman pushed him, and he hit the mirror.

Glass shattered then something sharp dug into his skull.

"I'm bleeding!" Olivia shouted. "I'm bleeding!"

"Fuck. Call 911," the cameraman said.

"That's not you bleeding," the publicist said. "That's Logan."

Olivia was shouting at him not to call anyone, then the voices faded, and only the pain remained.

Maddie, he thought. *Maddie.*

And then there was...nothing.

***

The smell was gone. Dog was in the city now, and too many smells hid the man's scent.

A boy called to him in a coaxing voice. "Come over here, puppy. I'll feed you."

Dog ran from him. The boy smelled good, but he wasn't his human.

Later, when he was near the end of the city, a woman in a yard called out to him. "Food," she said, holding out a chunk of meat that made his mouth water. "Here, sweetie, here. I have food. I'll feed you."

He came close but not close enough for her to grab him.

She sighed and threw the meat at him. He gobbled it then ran off.

"Come back tomorrow!" she yelled after him, but he knew he wouldn't be back.

He was limping more than ever. Yet he ran, as he did every day, finding a rhythm that worked for him.

He thought maybe if he was high up, he could smell the man again. He remembered where the scent had come from and kept running in that direction.

Finally he was outside the city. Not hearing or smelling any people or animals nearby, he stopped to take bites of the cold snow and swallow until his belly was full. The sun was lowering, and soon he would have to find a spot to rest for the night. He ran along a road and was about to look for a safe place to sleep when he saw a hill. His back leg aching with every step, he ran up it until he reached the top.

From here, he should smell his human's scent.

He sniffed and sniffed and sniffed, going in a circle and then another and another. But still his human's smell eluded him. Finally, he stopped, his head lowered, admitting the truth. His human's scent had disappeared. It was as if he'd never been there, had never existed.

But he had been there. Dog knew it.

What had happened to the man? *What had happened?*

He lifted his nose, and he howled.

Other dogs howled back. He didn't know if they were looking for their humans or if they just liked to howl. He'd known dogs like that.

And he'd known humans like that.

When he stopped howling, he sniffed one last time. Still no smell of his human, but something else was there. Every time he'd sniffed his human, there had been another scent nearby. A woman's scent. That's what he smelled now.

If he found the woman, maybe he would find the

man.

He headed forward, looking for a place to curl up and sleep.

In the morning, he would run toward the scent of the woman.

He was closer to the scent now than before. Still far away but not as far as before.

He would find her. He had no other choice.

***

Maddie waited until Zach was sleeping before she hurried upstairs, her footsteps soft so she wouldn't wake him. Ginger followed her then dashed ahead. In Logan's grandmother's bedroom, Maddie looked around. The bed was unmade, the covers pushed to the side, as if he were going to come back any moment.

But when she checked the drawers and the closet, there was nothing of his left behind. Nothing.

She sat on the edge of the bed, and there was a heaviness in her chest. Her eyes burned, but she didn't cry. She refused to cry.

He was gone. After that woman.

Questions tumbled into her mind. Why hadn't she made love to him more often? She'd wanted to. She'd wanted him badly.

And he'd wanted her, too.

But, no, she'd been afraid of being hurt. Afraid of being left behind.

Yet she was left behind anyway.

Would she have felt any more hurt if she had made

love to him more than that one time?

Huffing a sigh, she curled onto the sheets he'd slept on, her head lying on the pillow he'd rested his head on.

It wasn't enough. She rolled onto her back and pulled up the sheets that had covered him.

Ginger jumped onto the bed and lay on the pillow above her head, her warm belly pressing against Maddie's crown.

She reached up to scratch Ginger's side. "Is this what you did with him?" she murmured. "Curl up against his head?"

Ginger answered with a meow that Maddie took for a yes.

The ceiling light shone down on them. She put her hand down and lay like that for a long time. Finally she sighed. Ginger jumped away from her before she got up, though Maddie didn't know how Ginger knew she was going to roll out of bed. But it wasn't the first time Ginger had done that, and Maddie thought it was a cat thing.

Or else she just had a brilliant cat, something she already knew.

Instead of leaving right away, she stripped the bed of the sheets and pillowcases.

She set her lips together. She would not come back the next day and moon over him.

Holding the sheets against her chest, she went downstairs.

When Zach had asked when Logan would be back, she'd said she didn't know.

Now she knew. He was with his dark queen, under her spell again.

He would never come back.

If Zach asked about Logan tomorrow, she would have to tell him that she didn't expect Logan back again.

They were on their own again, and she had no reason to feel weepy. To feel as if she'd miss him in ways that she'd never missed Zach's father. In the short time Logan had been in their house—his house, really—with his cynicism and his smile and his sharp eyes that saw everything, he'd seen through her barriers and had become part of their lives. He'd snuck his way into her heart, and now it felt...empty. Dull. Tender.

Broken.

But he'd never made any promises, and she'd always known this day was going to come.

She'd just hoped it wouldn't.

Hope had made a damn fool of her, and she wouldn't allow it to happen again.

Her footsteps dragging, her spine bent slightly, because she felt bent and crooked, she went into the basement, which was about ten degrees colder than the upstairs, and dumped the bedding into a laundry basket. She was tempted to wash them right now—wash away any evidence that he'd been there—but that wouldn't take away the dullness in her chest.

Instead, she headed upstairs. She needed to do something. Things were happening to her, and for once, she needed to be the one who made things happen.

When she reached the first floor, she called Patty Kohlman. Patty answered on the second ring.

"I need to meet with you." Maddie sagged into the recliner Logan had sat in so often. It had been her recliner before he came. Now it was hers again. She was reclaiming it. "Tomorrow. And any other members who can make it."

"We know about the recall. We contacted a lawyer about it already."

"Did you see the lawyer yet?"

"Not yet." Patty's voice was flat.

"Neither have I. But if the board doesn't talk to me, not only will you waste your money paying a lawyer for something you won't win, but you and the board members are going to look like either fools or co-conspirators."

"Are you threatening us?"

"No, Patty, I'm telling you the truth, and I'm not sure if you know what the truth is. Do you know the reason Duane was fired?"

"Do you really have to do this?"

"No, I could sit here like a mouse and agree with everything you do. But I'm not a mouse."

Seconds of silence came from the other end. Maddie forced herself not to say anything first, remembering a saying she'd heard that the one who speaks first loses.

"Duane was very upfront about it. He made a mistake," Patty said in the same flat tone. "He made a mistake with a woman who worked in the town hall. His wife forgave him, but because of the circumstances, he decided the best thing to do was to leave."

"*He* decided?" Maddie asked.

"Yes, he did. Now, is that all? Anything else you have to say can be said tomorrow. I'll be there. I don't like the ugly way everything is going."

"Ugly acts get ugly results, Patty."

"We were helping a friend."

Now it was Maddie's turn to be silent. Patty's comment told her the board didn't consider her to be a friend.

Did that make them her enemies?

"I'll see if any of the other board members will come. I'm not sure if I should tell George and Duane or not."

"Go ahead, but in that case, it will be an official meeting. I'll make sure everything is recorded. In fact, that's a good idea, in any case. Be at my office at ten a.m. tomorrow." When she hung up, her hands were shaking. She wondered if she would sleep tonight.

23

At ten minutes to ten the next morning, Patty called to tell her the meeting was off. Instead, they'd made an appointment to see the lawyer.

"Are you charging the town?" Maddie asked.

The silence on the other end told Maddie that the answer to her question was a yes. Patty didn't want to confirm it, yet since Maddie was the one who would process the paperwork, she couldn't lie to her.

The way she'd been lied to already.

"The fact is," Patty said, her deep voice sharp, "that a man with more experience and with lifelong ties to the community was available, and we'd be doing the people of the town a disservice not to hire him."

"The problem is that you don't have the facts."

"Duane made a mistake, and he's deeply sorry for what he's done. He's human. He's fallible. He's—"

"A liar," Maddie said. "I'm not saying there wasn't an affair, but that's not the reason Duane was fired. You might want to double-check your facts, because George and Duane are making fools out of you. And in return, you and other town board members have made a fool out of me. No more, Patty. No more."

She hung up.

Her hand shook. How did a year that had started off with so much promise gotten so ugly?

She hadn't gotten the job she was promised.

She'd been lied to. She'd been cheated out of a job.

She'd lost income she could have been earning because she hadn't looked for a different job.

She'd met a man she...

Well, she'd met a man.

He'd left for another woman.

She closed her eyes tightly, and her hands on her desk cramped into fists. Inside, her belly was a hot, tight mass of anger, and in her heart, she sorrowed.

She clamped her mouth shut to hold back a cry, and on her comfortable office chair, she rocked back and forth, back and forth, back and forth, until an odd noise stopped her.

Her eyes snapped open even as she recognized the grinding sound of her coffeemaker. Efficient as usual, she'd prepared it ahead of time this morning to start at ten a.m.

At least she could count on something, she thought.

Then she took a deep breath. And another. And a third.

There didn't seem to be much to be grateful for, but she couldn't function like this all day. It would eat a hole in her heart or in her soul that would fill with bitterness. Already, she felt the poison eating at her insides.

She needed to start her list of the good things that had happened this last year.

Immediately, thoughts rushed into her mind too fast to assign numbers or even her beloved bullet points.

She and Zach were healthy. She had her master's degree. Zach's teacher loved him. She had friends who were rooting for her.

She hadn't gotten arrested for trespassing and

squatting.

And after five years of abstinence, she'd had sex. And not just sex in small, everyday letters. She'd had SEX. WOW SEX. WONDERFUL SEX. FAN-FUCKING-TASTIC SEX.

So he'd left her for another woman. So what? He'd never made promises to her. In fact, she was the one who had pulled back.

And as for him leaving...it was his loss. She would get over him. It might take a while, though she wasn't planning on waiting five years again.

And as for the house... She would leave soon.

And as for the town board... She wasn't going to get bitter.

She was going to get even.

Or maybe not. She wasn't sure that was good karma. Getting even might leave the stomach-twisting bitterness inside her, and she didn't want that. But neither was she going to be the town board's doormat. She wasn't going to meekly turn her back after they stomped over her. That wasn't good karma for her or for them.

It made her wonder who else they'd been stomping over.

The door between her office and the outer one opened, and Caroline stuck her head in. "Need anything before the big meet?"

"It was called off."

Caroline's eyebrows shot up, wrinkles creasing her forehead.

"They're seeing a lawyer," Maddie said.

"Because of the recall?" Caroline's eyebrows

contracted, vertical creases added to the horizontal ones.

Maddie twisted her lips. When one lawyer became involved, more lawyers often followed. And Caroline and Maddie's other supporters wouldn't be able to charge the town for their costs.

She looked down at the manila envelope. "The board members didn't want to see this, but I think you'll find it interesting reading. Why don't you grab a cup of coffee and take a look?"

Caroline didn't need another invitation, hurrying to the coffeemaker. While she was getting her cup, Maddie checked her private email to see if there was anything from her sister....

Though even as she thought that, she knew she was lying. It wasn't her sister whose name she was looking for.

His name wasn't there. But something else was. An email from Bert's investigative agency. She'd sent the company a resume after she'd gotten back from the luncheon, then so much had happened that she'd forgotten about it.

She clicked it open, but before she got a chance to read it, Caroline sat in front of her, holding her mug that said "Wine is always better than Whine" with both hands, her expression making Maddie think of a mischievous cat. "Here I am. What's the scoop? The dirtier the better."

Maddie's stomach tightened and so did her clutch on the envelope. For a moment, she couldn't talk.

"My stomach." Maddie felt her stomach clutching. "It's telling me not to do this."

"My stomach tells me to eat candy and ice cream all day."

"My stomach tells me the same thing, but this is different. I'm just not sure I should do this." She looked down at the envelope, not understanding why she wasn't giving it to Caroline.

"You're too nice." Caroline got up. "You don't know how to be mean."

"My sister says the same thing." They were right. She knew it. She wanted to give it to Caroline. The town deserved to know the truth.

Yet her stomach coiled even tighter, and she pulled the envelope over her belly.

"And you know what happens to nice girls?" Caroline asked.

"They don't have fun?"

"They try to please everyone." Picking up her coffee, she turned to leave. "And they end up pleasing no one. Especially not themselves."

Watching her leave, Maddie's stomach clutched even tighter, so she bent forward over the desk. She suspected she was wrong with her interpretation of what her stomach was telling her. That it was really telling her that Caroline was right.

And why was she listening to her stomach? Her mind knew for certain that Caroline was right.

Yet she didn't go after Caroline. Instead she straightened and put the manila envelope in a drawer...and locked it.

***

"I feel awful." Kris's voice over the phone was wobbly, and Maddie imagined her wringing her hands.

"You are awful," Maddie said in the back hall of her house, taking off her jacket with one hand and holding her phone with the other because the speakerphone echoed in the small place. She'd already phoned Kris at her break, keeping her up to date on the county board train wreck.

Now Kris was sharing her own bad news.

This day kept getting worse. She imagined that if she looked up the December horoscope for Virgo, it would have a thick, black X over it.

A meow brought her attention downward, and Ginger twirled around her ankles. She sighed and bent to pet her with her free hand, scratching Ginger's neck. "Just kidding. I understand perfectly that Cody's parents want you to visit with them on Christmas."

"We told him we'd come early next year—I'm not looking forward to flying over the holidays—but they sent us the tickets." The resentment in her voice made Maddie wince. Clearly, the Gemini horoscope, her sister's sign, didn't have a happy face, either.

"Yeah, well..."

"And I know what a crappy time this is for you," Kris continued. "I almost feel like telling Cody to go without me."

Maddie slipped off her coat and sat on the kitchen chair, still wearing her boots as it had snowed another inch this afternoon. But Ginger jumped on her lap and began kneading happily, and petting her was more important than worrying about a little snow on the floor.

"Ack," Kris said. "That's enough of my shitty day. What about yours?"

"Guess what I'm going to do very soon?"

"What?"

"You know that saying about one door closing and another opening?"

"Are you talking about Christmas? You're invited someplace else?"

"It's more important than that. Besides, Ginger will like having us home for once." Bending to peer into Ginger's green eyes, she lowered her voice. "Won't you, sweetie pie?"

"She's not your baby."

"If you had a cat, you'd change your mind. There's a reason people call them fur babies."

"The reason is that people are soft in the heads. Anyway, what door is opening?"

"I have an interview! January second."

"No kidding. Where?"

"Remember I told you about the detective agency that I sent my resume to? It's them."

"You said it's in Minnesota." Kris made the four-syllable state a whine.

"I know. Isn't it great that it's so close?"

"It's a two-hour drive each way."

"An hour and a half drive. Though maybe the way you drive it's longer, Mrs. Turtle."

"Ha ha ha."

"No, it's ho ho ho. And no whining, please." Her voice cracked. The effort to put up a cheerful front was too much, and her hold on Ginger tightened. "I can't take it anymore."

The cat meowed her complaint and jumped off, hurrying away from her, making her feel guilty for holding her too tightly.

"You didn't hear from Logan?"

"No."

"I looked him up a few times today. I didn't see anything."

"Me, too." She'd Googled Olivia's name, too, and hated everything she read, though there wasn't anything new.

"I'm sorry."

"I'm not. It's good that I learned this now." Not that he'd promised her anything. And she'd said she wouldn't hope…but she'd stupidly hoped anyway. "I'd better go. Remember, no whining, okay?"

"Got it. If you can get through this without whining, so can I. If there's any news about anything, let me know. Anything at all. And call anytime."

"I will."

"Except Saturday night between eight and nine p.m."

Maddie laughed. "I'll put that on my calendar. 'K & C's Nookie Time.'"

"I might be packing this Saturday. Hard to believe Christmas is coming so soon. Less than a week."

Maddie agreed, and they said good-bye. Moving slowly, she put on her slippers then started her dinner. For a short time, every day had seemed special. Magical. Now the days seemed gray, except for the times she was with Zach.

She stepped into the living room and looked out the

big picture window, in the direction of California. "Come back," she said softly. "Come back to me."

Her words hung in the air, like vibrations from a tuning fork. She waited a moment, as if she were expecting a reply, which would've been cute but didn't happen. Of course it didn't.

But it wouldn't hurt to say one more thing, and this she said loudly, almost shouting:

"I still have more stories to tell."

Then she turned and strode to the bedroom to change out of her work clothes and, after that, start dinner.

She'd done all that she could do...except call him and tell him. But she couldn't do that. She would not beg him to come back. It had to be his choice.

***

Logan thrashed, swimming through a thick blackness, trying to get up, but a pressure kept pushing him down, down, down.

It wasn't water, because he could breathe, but he seemed to have lost his strength. He kicked his legs and paddled his arms and hands...and nothing happened.

He must have made some progress. A shape appeared ahead of him. He called out, wanting the shape to turn. It seemed important that he see what it was.

He called and called and called...

The shape turned. A medium-sized, mostly brown dog with white on his face and fur that looked like long pieces of yarn. A dog of mixed breed, definitely one-of-a-kind.

His heart leapt.

Einy! It was Einy!

His dog who'd died so long ago was here, in this black ether, waiting for him.

"Einy!" he shouted. "Einy!"

Einy turned back and paddled away from him. Panic made him shout Einy's name again as he swam after him. "Einy, don't go! Come back, Einy!"

But Einy continued on, not hearing him. If Einy had heard him, he would dog-paddle back instead of away.

"Einy!" he screamed. "Einy! Einy! Einy!"

Someone was clutching his hands, but he couldn't see who it was. "Einy!"

A wave of tiredness pushed through him, and it wasn't right. Wasn't natural. Someone was drugging him to keep him from Einy.

"EINEEEEEEEEE!" he screamed one last time, the sound echoing inside his head as the ether swallowed him up and drowned him.

**

Dog was sleeping on a back porch, curled tightly to stay as warm as he could, the house blocking the freezing north wind, when the dream started. He was in the water, and his human was calling his name. *"Einy! Einy! Einy! Einy!"*

He tried to swim toward his human, but he was being pulled in another direction.

And finally he was swimming away as his human called his name again, "Einy!"

He whimpered, his feet moving, deep in the black sleep, and finally the pressure that kept him facing forward went away, and he turned...

To nothingness... His human was no longer there.

But there was some consolation. Now he had a name.

Einy.

24

The week heading up to Christmas felt to Maddie a crappy time to have her life fall apart. It was the second time it'd happened to her. But she couldn't feel sorry for herself. Instead of feeling sad, she was starting to get angry. Angry at the board. Angry at George and Duane. Angry at Logan and his dark queen—which she always thought was a stupid name for the actress. As if the woman had mythical powers over him.

"Bitch" would've been so much better.

But sadness simmered beneath the anger. Not the best combination for Christmas cheer.

Every year since Maddie had started working for the town hall, they were allowed to pipe music through the speakers for the holiday season. Caroline chose a country music station, and at least once a day, Maddie heard Dolly Parton's "Hard Candy Christmas."

A great way to describe her Christmas. She scowled a lot at work, though at home she had to keep up her smile for Zach. He was moping because Logan was gone, and she didn't want to make it worse.

And then the day before Christmas, Patty and the three male board members walked into her office to ask her not to take her "disappointment" out on the town.

Anger fired up inside her, so fast and so hot she shook with it. She clenched her teeth and curled her hands into fists, and the anger grew more and more intense.

Enough with being understanding. Enough with

being the good guy. Enough, enough, enough. What had all her understanding and goodness gotten her? Not the job she'd been promised. Not money. Not even honesty.

She shot up to her feet and leaned over her desk toward them. "You broke a promise to me. And you know what's worse?" She paused and took in the fear that flicked across their faces. Too late to be afraid, she thought. The dam had broken, and they were about to be flooded with her ire. "You broke your promise to the town to do the best for them. You don't even want to know the real reason Duane lost his job. So far, I've been hesitant to stir anything up. But that's done now."

"Maddie." Patty held out her hand. "Don't—"

"No!" Maddie slammed her fist on the desktop, and Kevin Spindlebottom jumped. "You've lost my respect. I'm moving on. Happy Christmas to you. I'm handing the information to the townspeople. As for myself, I'm seriously considering suing you."

"You'd be suing the town," Patty said, but her eyes were wide, her shoulders stiff.

"Would I? I'm not sure. Knowing what I know and what you've ignored, it's possible the town might be able to sue you for your decision."

Still caught up in the anger, it gave her a sense of satisfaction to see their faces blanch.

"I want you to leave." She pointed at the doorway and didn't care that her hand shook.

They turned, as if in a daze, and they slunk out. And good riddance to all four of them, she thought viciously, including Barney, who owned the wine shop in town.

From now on, she'd buy her cheap wine at the grocery

store.

The door between her office and the outer office opened. "I hope you really do sue them," Caroline said.

Maddie gazed at her, unable to say anything as her body trembled and she took deep breaths.

Elvis was crooning "Blue Christmas" over the speakers, and Caroline added, "I'd like to see their Christmases turn blue with worry."

"Me, too." Maddie's voice quavered. "I shouldn't be vindictive, but they deserve to suffer."

"I hope you'll give me what you have."

"You first."

"What did Duane do? Are you ready to tell me now? Sexual harassment?"

"I wouldn't doubt it, but all I have is embezzlement."

"Shit."

"Yeah, shit."

"Is that in the envelope?"

Maddie nodded. "If you really want to read it, you can."

"You bet I do. I'm proud of you today. You can be nice and still kick butt."

Maddie laughed but heard an edge of hysteria and clamped her lips tighter.

"There's no way the town will let an embezzler be the administrator," Caroline said. "You know how the townspeople are about money. You're sure you won't take the position?"

"Not a chance." The position would be poisoned to her now.

Caroline sighed. "I wish you'd change your mind. Or

run for the town board. You'd be elected in a minute."

She shook her head. In the new year, she'd be gone. Funny, she was back to where she'd been five years ago, ready to sleep in her sister's basement. But now Kris and Cody had put carpeting and a bar and even a guest bedroom in the basement. It would be fun, Kris had said over the phone.

But Maddie had hopes it wouldn't last long. She had a good feeling about her appointment with Bert next week to talk about the position at his investigative agency. And she probably wouldn't sue the town, but she could demand a settlement. They owed it to her. Perhaps there was a way they could get it from George and Duane, the original liars.

"At least you're not quitting until you have a new job," Caroline said. "For your sake, I hope you find one. But I've gotta admit, I'm going to miss you."

"I'll miss you, too," Maddie said, and her voice was almost steady now, just a little wobble. If it was just her, she would have left already. But she had to do what was best for Zach. "And until I get that wonderful job, I have to stay for the insurance."

Caroline sighed again, and Maddie silently agreed that insurance was something to sigh about. It wouldn't be long before she found a new job, she promised herself.

"Don't give me your sad face," she said, putting on her own happy face that she'd created for the times when she wanted to slam her fist against a wall, over and over and over. Her fake-it-until-you-believe-it face. "I have my present for you."

They had both bought Wisconsin wine for a gift this

year. Door County cranberry wine for Caroline and a dry Riesling from Prairie du Sac for Maddie. They hugged. No one was coming to the town hall on Christmas Eve day. Next week would be their busy time, with people dropping in to pay their taxes. But today it was dead enough for them to dance when Brenda Lee sang "Rock Around the Clock" over the speakers, with Caroline showing off her fancy moves.

When the clock clicked at four p.m., they had their jackets and were ready to lock up and hurry outside. They'd already hugged good-bye inside, and they rushed out to their cars, holding their wine bottles to their chests, as well as their knit hats on their heads, otherwise the wicked wind coming from the north would whip them right off.

As Maddie scrambled into her SUV, she imagined that Logan's dark queen would never wear a cranberry knit hat—especially one that the cat had been sitting on in the morning.

Maddie wasn't so picky. She stopped off at Zach's friend's house to collect him and wish the family a Merry Christmas. She gave them the bottle of wine that Caroline had given her and thanked them for taking care of Zach.

Then she and Zach rushed into the wicked wind again, and she was glad, so glad, that she and Zach had a warm home to go to.

"Mommy?"

He was sitting in his car seat in the back. She glanced in the rearview mirror, though she didn't have a good view of him. "What, honey?"

"Is Logan coming?"

The three words pierced the I'm-doing-fabulous mask she'd been wearing since she'd picked him up. Her breath stuck in her chest, and she pressed her lips together to keep from crying out in pain.

"Mommy?"

Her breath shuddered out. "No, sweetheart, he won't be here. But that's okay. We have each other. And we have Ginger."

"The real Christmas is tomorrow. I think he'll come for Christmas. In my letter to Santa, I wished that Logan would stay and be my daddy."

She clutched the steering wheel. "Honey, Santa gives toys. He doesn't send people into your life."

"I asked God, too. Every night I ask him."

A ball of emotion blocked her throat as she steered into the driveway of her temporary home. And then the ball shrank, but she still didn't say anything. As if she secretly expected that maybe God had heard Zach. That maybe God had answered him. That when she reached the house, she would see a rental car parked in front of it.

But when they drove down the tree-lined lane past her house to the garage, there was no vehicle waiting for them.

She pressed the garage door opener. "Zach, I don't think—"

"Mommy! I prayed."

Her eyes closed as the garage door rolled up. "Just don't be too hurt if he doesn't come." She turned around, and in the dim light, she saw his mouth set in a stubborn line.

She turned back and drove into the garage. Nothing she could say would stop him from hoping. And nothing she could do would stop him from heartbreak. Not when he was only four years old. And it didn't get better at twenty-seven. Not for her, anyway.

As she unclicked her seat belt, took the key out of the ignition, then got out of the car, she admitted the truth to herself.

She'd fallen a little in love with Logan.

Oh crap, she was still lying. She'd fallen all the way in love with him. Like Jill tumbling down the hill after Jack. She was no better than that. In fact, she'd dived in without taking a deep breath first—and drowned in love.

And now he was gone, and she hadn't heard from him. But she was still breathing, her damaged heart was still beating, and blood was still pulsing through her veins.

She would survive, and she would heal. Someday.

Zach scrambled out of the car seat, and she bent to lift him out, though he was getting too big. She hugged him tightly before putting him down to collect his backpack with a gift from his friend.

They ran from the unattached garage to the house, their heads down, and Maddie told herself she should be happy they had a warm house to go to, even though it was temporary. So many people didn't even have that, and she felt for them.

Even with everything that had happened, she had her son and a warm place to stay. She was the lucky one.

***

Dog was cold, so cold. Cold all the way through his skin, his muscles, his bones. He limped along the highway, pain knifing through his leg with every step, his body weak.

There had been no food lately, no small animals to eat. They were hiding in their warm places, sleeping, staying away from predators like him.

Dog kept moving because movement kept him warmer than if he stopped.

If he lay down, he would die.

Cars whizzed by, most of them veering away from him, but some driving so close the draft of icy wind ruffled his fur and even his skin that had gotten loose.

One car, though, stopped.

He stopped, too, his back bowed against the wicked gusts, his body shivering.

Voices and smells came to him. There was a girl and a man and a woman. The girl was crying, and then the woman was saying something that the man didn't like. Dog could tell the woman was the dominant one, and then the door opened and she stepped out, covered by clothes, but Dog could tell by her smell that she was female.

The woman held out her hands. "Are you lost? You look like you're starving. It's Christmas Eve, and we can't leave you out in the cold."

Dog stepped toward her. His human was gone, and if he didn't go with the woman...he would die.

He couldn't jump into their car; his leg hurt too badly. The lady lifted him in, making a grunting noise. She sat in the back with him, telling the girl not to touch him until she had time to check and see what was wrong with him.

At the house, the woman put Dog in a porch with walls and a door but no heat. She kept him for a moment while she ran in the house and then came out with food that he gobbled up. After that, he wanted to lie down and sleep, but the lady took a scissors. Kneeling on the cold floor, she cut his tangled fur, talking softly to him the whole time. Twice she found a spot that made him flinch, places where he'd been hurt, and she crooned over them.

Finally she got to her feet and said he was good. Then they went into the house, where warm air settled around him like a blanket. There was a bowl of water by the refrigerator, and he craned his head down to the bowl and drank while the girl and the lady watched him. As he finished, the lady told the girl the word he didn't like: *Bath.*

The girl scampered out of the kitchen, and a moment later, he wasn't surprised to hear water running.

"Come," the woman said. "Come."

Because she'd fed and watered him, he followed her and let the lady give him a bath. Then the girl came in and rubbed him dry with the towel. He liked that, pressing his body against hers. It felt like a long time since a human had rubbed him.

"Look, he's a beauty," the woman said.

"I love him." The girl kissed his head above his ear, and he opened his mouth and panted at her. He liked her. She was young, but not so young as to poke him in his eye and pull his tail.

He heard the man coming down the steps, the sound

heavy and his smell heavy, too.

"I asked for a dog from Santa." The girl kissed his head again before turning to her mom. "Can I keep him, Mom?"

The dad groaned. "I knew this would happen."

The mom laughed and went over and hugged him. His arms went around her, too. Dog leaned his head against the girl.

His human was gone. The girl wasn't his human, but she was here, and she wanted him.

If he found the woman who'd been with his human, she might not want him.

How could he take that chance?

25

It was a good morning for Dog—in the beginning. Though the man didn't like him, the girl kept hugging and kissing him. The woman liked him, too. She gave him more food and water. The humans ate different food, but the girl gave him some under the table. The woman did the same thing.

After that, the humans gave gifts to each other. The girl said her best gift was Dog, though she called him a name he didn't like. But she gave him more food, so he didn't mind if she called him the wrong name.

The woman was busy cleaning. Dog knew what that meant. Humans liked to clean. They did it all the time.

The girl sat in the room with a TV and a tree. She played with a game she held on her lap, and it had pictures that moved. Dog lay down by her feet and thought she'd have more fun taking him for a walk, but not when it was so cold outside. So he rested his head on his paws, watching the woman pick up all the paper while the man did something in the kitchen.

A car pulled into the driveway. Dog jumped to his feet, even though his sore leg hurt, and barked to warn them. The woman looked outside and shouted, "They're here! They're here!"

The man yelled, "Will someone shut the dog up?"

"Dad!" the girl said. "Don't yell at Rocky." She got down on her knees next to him and hugged him. "Shhh. It's just Grandma and Grandpa."

Dog whimpered. It wasn't just Grandma and Grandpa. Someone else was with them, too. Dog smelled it. Dog heard it.

It'd happened to him at the last place, and it was happening to him again.

The woman opened the door, and cold air rushed in then a man and woman, laughing, and the woman was holding something in her arms, something fuzzy and squirming and making a whining sound. "Heidi, guess what we got for you for Christmas?"

"A puppy!" The girl ran from Dog to the puppy, holding it, cooing over it, kissing it. The puppy was little, and she licked the girl's face, and the girl laughed. "Can I name it?"

"She's your puppy," the grandmother said. "You can name her anything you want."

"She's brown like cocoa. I'm going to name her Coco. I love her already." She looked at Dog and said she loved him, too. But all the time, she held the squirmy puppy, laughing because she was licking her jaw.

She was the puppy's human. Not Dog's.

"You knew about this?" the girl's mom asked the girl's dad.

"It's why I didn't want another dog. I wanted to surprise both of you."

"Well, now we have two."

"Let's see how it goes. Maybe we can keep both dogs." But the man's voice was flat.

"I think we should keep both dogs." The woman looked him in the eyes. "After all, this is Christmas."

They kissed then, and Dog got to his feet. He

suspected that what the woman said was what would happen. In every tribe, there was an alpha dog, and in this house, it was the woman.

He had a home here. It wasn't far from where he'd smelled the woman who'd been with his human. He could go outside every day, and if he smelled his human, he could leave.

Until then, he should stay and be warm and fed and have his leg heal.

Dog walked to the door, and the girl's grandpa said, "I'll let him outside." He opened the door, and the woman yelled, "No! Put him in the back, with the fence."

The grandpa started to close the door, but Dog was raising his nose, sniffing the air. The woman's scent came to him, and in that instant, he made his decision.

He darted past the grandfather, into the cold, the door hitting his back leg, the one that was hurt. He yelped then his feet hit the sidewalk, and he ran from the house as fast as he could with his injured leg.

***

There was an ache in Maddie's throat all day, and her cheek muscles hurt from smiling. She and Zach had breakfast then opened presents and kissed and laughed then went to church where she hugged friends and avoided the board members who avoided her back. She stayed for the buffet, for which she'd brought brownies that she'd made last night. Zach played with his friends, and she heard him laughing once in a while, easily picking out his voice from all the others. Every time, it eased the ache in her throat, but the good feeling didn't last long.

When they left, only about twenty other cars were in the parking lot. As they drove to their house, Zach said, "Mom, I want to call Logan."

"Oh, honey. He's far away."

"I want to call him."

She glanced at him and saw his mouth was stubborn. When he got like that, he wouldn't budge. Her father, who she'd talked to last night, was like that, too.

"Please let me call him?"

"Maybe I should call him. Wait until we get home, okay?"

"Okay."

They reached home, and Zach ignored all the toys and electronic gifts. She'd gone overboard with the Christmas toys; she always did. Kris liked to say she was making up for not having a father around. Or grandparents. Both her parents sent money for Zach, but that went straight into his college fund.

Inside the house, she made him wait while she put away their jackets and mittens and hats. Then she put her empty brownie pan in the sink and filled it with warm water. She wanted to tell Zach to wait until they changed to their comfortable shoes, but when she turned from the sink, he was jumping with impatience.

She sat at the kitchen table with her phone. She'd hoped Zach would have been diverted by his toys, but when he wanted something badly, not much could divert him.

She found Logan's number in her cell phone

directory. As she pressed on it, she realized how tense she was, all her muscles tightened.

It rang four times, then a woman's neutral voice gave her the "mailbox is full" message. She told Zach, whose shoulders slumped.

In that second, she hated Logan. It was bad enough he'd made her fall in love with him—yes, in love, she admitted to herself. She was strong, though, and someday she would get past it. But he was breaking her son's heart, too. Damn him for that.

"Mom, I want to text him."

"Honey, he's—"

"Please, Mom. He'll answer me. I know he will."

She didn't reply right away, gripping the phone, looking into his eyes, knowing that whatever she did would lead to heartache.

But if she said no, he would always believe he might have had a chance. His heart would still be bruised, but added to the hurt would be resentment aimed at her.

She handed him the phone. "Will you need help?" He knew how to read already—he was very smart for his age—but she wasn't sure about his spelling abilities.

He shrugged and with one finger typed letters in slowly then held it up to her. "Is this right?"

She bent forward to read it. *i mis u come hom*

Tears pricked her eyes. "It's wonderful," she said, her voice husky. She pointed. "You press this."

"I know that," he said, as if he knew everything at four and one-half years old, and he sent the message.

They waited, though she suspected it wouldn't go through. She'd never had her voice mail so full it wouldn't take messages, but she was pretty sure if her voice mail wouldn't go through, neither would—

A message popped up: *look out the door. im here.*

Raising her head, she felt lightheaded. She started to shake as Zach sounded out the words one by one, doing well until he got to "im," calling it "in."

She put her hand on his shoulder. "Honey, he's outside."

His eyes opened wide, then he dropped the phone on her lap and ran to the side door, shouting, "Logan! Logan! Logan!"

She set the phone on the table and walked slowly behind him. He whipped open the door and held up his arms. From where she stood, she could see a hand grip Zach on each side of his ribs. Laughing, Logan raised him up high.

Her heart, which had felt shrunken and cold since he'd left, expanded and warmed.

"I *knew* you'd come," Zach said. "I made a special wish to Santa."

"That I'd come for Christmas?"

Zach shook his head. Even just looking at the back of his head, Maddie knew he was beaming at Logan, love pouring out of his eyes. "That you'd be my daddy."

***

"You'd better take your suitcase in." Maddie took Zach from Logan and let her shiny-eyed son onto the hall floor.

How was she supposed to tell her son that he

shouldn't say what he'd just said?

She couldn't. Instead, she kissed his forehead and whispered that she loved him.

"I love you, too, Mom." He wheeled around. "And I love Logan, too."

Logan put his hand on Zach's shoulder. "Right back at you, big boy."

Zach beamed at him. "I am big. Bigger than all the boys in my class."

"That is big. And the girls, too, right?"

"Two girls are bigger." Zach held up two fingers in a vee.

"Logan..." She stared at him. In the light of the kitchen, she saw his face was drawn and his complexion sallow.

His smile was wary. "Hello, Maddie."

"I was worried about you," Maddie said, almost in a whisper. "You look tired, and—" She frowned. Something was wrong with his hair on his left side. It sat funny. She raised her hand to push his hair back, and she saw a shaved area and what looked like a red ridge about an inch long and one-half inch wide.

Fear buzzed inside her heard. "What happened?"

"A mirror broke."

"On your *head*?"

He nodded.

"Was Olivia involved? Your dark queen?"

"You're full of suspicions."

"You're not answering my question." She was aware of Zach looking from her to Logan.

"The dark queen is no longer my queen."

Tears rose in her eyes. She turned her face away from him, down at Zach, who stared at her with his eyes big and scared.

"Mommy! You're crying!"

"I'm fine, I'm fine, I'm fine." She wiped tears away, but more were flowing out.

"Do you mind if I talk to your mom alone?" Logan said, his voice low. "I have something to tell her that I hope will make her happy."

"*I* can make her happy. She's *my* mom."

"Maybe I can talk to her about your wish to Santa."

"You mean..."

"Be your daddy, right?"

Tears were running out of her eyes like a waterfall now. She needed a Kleenex but grabbed a napkin off the table instead. How could he say something like that to Zach? How dare he raise his hopes like that?

"I'm going to play with my new fire truck," Zach said loudly and happily. "In my bedroom."

"A great idea."

Giggling, Zach ran off, his footsteps pounding on the floor.

She blew her nose and watched Zach between furious blinks, her back to Logan.

"Will you turn around?" Logan asked, his voice low. "I have something for you."

Reminding herself that this emotional person wasn't her, that she was the one who plowed through problems until they were fixed, no matter how complicated, she turned around, prepared to be practical again.

He was holding something out to her in his palm. She

glanced down and gasped. A diamond ring. Beautiful and sparkling...and big. Very big.

"Will you marry me?" he asked.

"Oh my." She stared, her tears dried. Then she shook her head and forced her gaze from the ring to his face. "This is so...crazy. You don't know me."

"I know you. I know you by your stories. I know you by your heart." His blue eyes glowed brighter that the diamonds on the ring. "I know you by your actions. By the way you are with Zach. And you know me."

She glanced away from his eyes, downward, and saw he was clenching the ring in his hand now. An insane thought entered her mind, and wonder shivered through her.

He was afraid she'd say no.

"Maybe that's what's scaring you off," he said. "You know I'm not a prize."

"Are you kidding me?" She snapped her gaze up. "Most women would think you're the grand prize."

"Maybe, but you're not most women." His arm slid around her shoulder, and he smiled down at her. "You know my faults. I can be arrogant."

She nodded. True. "Irritatingly arrogant."

"I can be bullheaded."

She nodded harder. "Worse than a bull."

"I can be secretive."

She bit her lip. That part hurt.

"I can't promise to change all that. But the secretive part... That's gone."

"Just like that?" She stared at his face, trying to read his thoughts and feelings in his eyes, his mouth, the firm set of his jaw.

He snapped his fingers. "Like that. Once I make up my mind, I do it. That's one of my good points—and sometimes one of my bad ones. I'm also loyal. I'm a one-woman guy, and now I've found the right woman."

"Because I'm decent and good? The opposite of the dark queen?"

"This has nothing to do with her." His mouth lifted into a smile that was so tender her heart hurt. "It's because you're funny, you're strong, you tell a great story, you're an adequate cook—"

"What? I'm a great cook."

"A little delusional," he continued, as if she hadn't interrupted, "and you're amazing in bed."

"True. The last, I mean."

His eyes turned a dark blue. "And you love me."

"You say that, but you didn't call me," she whispered. "I thought I might never see you again."

"I was in the hospital overnight. Then I had to recuperate. I didn't want to worry you. While I was at it, I took care of business."

She raised her hand and cupped it over the wound. "She did this, didn't she? Olivia."

"Not on purpose."

Hot anger knifed through her. "I want to hurt her. You said it's nothing to do with her, but you left because you loved her. How could you come back now and say you love me?"

"I didn't love her when I left you. I went because she told me she was dying." His eyes didn't leave her face, compelling her to listen to him, to believe him. "We had a history together, and I went to be there for her, nothing else. I already knew that I didn't love her. I already knew in my heart that the woman I loved was you."

She closed her eyes. She wanted to believe him. Wanted it badly.

"I'm not pushing you to make a decision," he said. "I can wait."

Her eyes opened. "How long will you wait?"

"As long as it takes. I'm here for you for the duration, not just for right now. Till death do us part."

She laughed, but it came out like a sob. Clamping her mouth shut, she looked from him into the living room with the lighted, decorated tree and the corner filled with Zach's Christmas presents. And she thought of the way Logan had stuck to Olivia, even though she didn't deserve his loyalty.

This was a man who would stay by her.

She and he were so different—but that way they were both alike.

Still staring at the living room, she started to make a list in her head of the reasons she should marry him and the reasons she shouldn't. But she only got to the first three of the "should marry him" list: She loved him, Zach loved him, he loved her and Zach.

"Yes," she said, turning back to him.

"Yes what?"

"Yes, I'll marry you."

He grinned, he laughed, he put both arms around her. With a laugh low in her throat, she went up on her tiptoes and pressed her body against his. "Kiss me, you crazy fool."

"A fool in love," he said, and then his mouth was against hers, and she melted against him. Happiness sang through her, all her senses were alive and feeling...everything.

He pulled away first. "I love you."

"It's a good thing, because I love you, too."

They grinned at each other, and she went up higher on her tiptoes, and he bent his head lower. A soft "aaaaaah" sound came from her mouth. Their lovemaking had been spectacular before. Tonight there would be fireworks.

"Mom?"

She whipped her arms down and jumped back while Logan casually turned to Zach, who was heading toward them, his forehead crinkled.

"Zach, do you still want me to be your dad?"

Zach nodded, the crinkles going away.

"I'll have to marry your mom to do that."

Zach nodded again, and Maddie thought he was holding his breath, waiting to hear what Logan would say next.

"I'll have to kiss her, too. That's what married people do. Is that okay?"

Zach beamed at him, and Maddie thought he smiled not just with his mouth and his eyes but with every pore in his body. "Yes," he said. "Then you'll be my dad."

"I already have a ring for her." Logan brought it out of his pocket. "I'm going to put it on now. Do you want to watch?"

Zach nodded again. "That means you'll be married soon."

"You want it done soon?" Holding her left hand, Logan looked into Maddie's eyes.

Her throat too tight to talk, she nodded.

With a smile, he slid it on. "I didn't buy you a Christmas present. I didn't have time."

"I didn't get you anything for Christmas, either." Hearing a noise, she frowned and looked toward the door. "Wait a minute. Something is scratching on the door."

***

Dog's body shook with a mixture of cold and excitement. He was here! Dog's human was here!

He'd been looking for his human for so long. Ever since he was a puppy, he'd known he had one human, and he'd known he would have to find him. And now he was so near.

When he'd smelled his human again, he'd been at the edge of the city, limping slowly and so cold he thought about dropping down in the snow and never getting up.

Then the smell came. Better than anything, even bacon.

The smell had moved, and so had Dog. His hunting instincts had told him that his human would be going to the woman. He'd started to run, his back leg hurting. At times, he'd slid, but each time, he'd caught this balance then continued to run toward the smell of the woman. And now he was here, breathing fast, his heart pounding as he waited to claim his human.

Footsteps were coming to the door now, and the smell

of the woman was sharper. Then she reached the door, fumbling with something on the other side, taking too long. Dog whimpered with anxiety.

Finally, the door opened, the woman looking above him. No doubt expecting another human.

Then she looked down. "What...? A dog?" She started to open the door, and the scent of his human became stronger. "Are you—"

Dog leaped up and rushed through the small opening, his body pushing it wider. The woman stumbled back against the wall as Dog limped as fast as he could down the hall toward the smell.

A man who'd been sitting down jumped up. His human!

"Einy? Oh my God, Einy!" The human knelt, and Dog barreled into him.

Einy. Now he remembered the dream he had. And he remembered even more.

The man fell to the floor, and his arms wrapped around Dog as he licked the man's face, his whole body wiggling. Everything was clear to him now.

He'd been with his human a long time ago. He didn't remember what had happened, why they'd separated, but they were together again. He and his human.

"Logan?" the woman asked, her voice soft.

"Mom," a boy's voice said, "it's a dog. Can we keep it?"

"I don't know," the woman said. "Logan, you tell us. You and the dog seem to know each other. Is the dog yours?"

Logan. The name came back to Einy, and he laid his

head against Logan's chest while Logan found the special spot beneath his ear.

"He looks just like Einstein. Exactly like him. Einy was my dog for three years when I was a little older than Zach. Then one day my mother told me we were moving to England, and we couldn't take Einy with us."

"I bet you were devastated."

"It was the first time my heart was broken." He breathed into Einy's face, and Einy lifted his head and licked his chin.

Logan laughed and cuddled him closer. Einy smelled a cat nearby. He looked sideways. An orange and white cat was staring at him. Not an angry look, just curious.

"I'll have to call the humane society to see if anyone's reported losing a dog with this description." Einy's human stopped talking to rub his other ear. "I know it can't really be Einy. This dog only looks a few years old, and Einy was run over when I was nine, but I could swear it's him. If no one is looking for him, what do you think about starting our family off with an extra member?"

Instead of answering, she sat on the floor next to the man and held out the back of her hand to Einy for him to sniff. When he was done, she petted him.

The boy knelt on Einy's other side, and he petted Einy, too, his smaller hand sliding along Einy's spine. Einy felt full. Not in his belly, but in his chest. He put his head back against Logan and let the love fill him.

"I think," the woman said, "that Einy will complete our family." She smiled at Einy's human. "And we'll still have enough love for more."

While Logan laughed at her, the boy hugged Einy. Remembering another small boy hugging him, Einy leaned against the boy, making them laugh as lights on the tree winked at them.

It had taken him a long time, but Einy was finally home.

Save a Cat, Feed a Dog, Read a Book

25¢ from every CHRISTMAS AT ANGEL LAKE book sold will go to the Washington County Humane Society in Wisconsin. 25¢ from every Rescued Hearts book sold will be donated to a rescue association. (The exception will be if a Rescued Hearts book is part of a box set.)

Stay updated on all of my releases and special sales by subscribing to my newsletter: www.edieramer.com/newsletter/

Acknowledgments

Once again, thank you to two amazing authors, Dale Mayer and Michelle Diener, for their wonderful advice. I also have three Amys to thank: Amy Remus of So Many Reads, for making sure the timeline was correct. Amy Knupp from Blue Otter Editing for being so good. And Amy Atwell from Author E.M.S. for her formatting services that saves my sanity.

It doesn't take a village, but it certainly takes the help of these wise women. I'm lucky to have all of them in my life.

About Edie Ramer

I'm funnier on the page than in real life. I'm a multiple award-winning writer. I live in southeastern Wisconsin with my husband, our dog, and one important cat.

In addition to my Rescued Hearts and Miracle Interrupted series, I'm published in paranormal and sci fi romance, plus a humorous mystery. I'm happy to be able to do what I love nearly every day.